Underclass

Underclass

B. T. Gorman

Winchester, UK
Washington, USA

First published by Roundfire Books, 2013
Roundfire Books is an imprint of John Hunt Publishing Ltd., Laurel House, Station Approach,
Alresford, Hants, SO24 9JH, UK
office1@jhpbooks.net
www.johnhuntpublishing.com
www.roundfire-books.com

For distributor details and how to order please visit the 'Ordering' section on our website.

Text copyright: B. T. Gorman 2012

ISBN: 978 1 78099 888 6

A CIP catalogue record for this book is available from the British Library.

Design: Stuart Davies

Printed and bound by CPI Group (UK) Ltd, Croydon, CR0 4YY

We operate a distinctive and ethical publishing philosophy in all
areas of our business, from our global network of authors to
production and worldwide distribution.

Acknowledgements

The author would like to thank the following people for their assistance with Underclass.

The lovely folks at Roundfire Books for their help with publishing the book, Portsmouth Central Library and Librarians everywhere for the use of their facilities and for their continuing struggle to preserve the great warehouses of public knowledge.

Portsmouth Coalition, Matt and the gang from The Milton Arms/The Barn in Portsmouth for all the beer and laughter, Dave Morris for his sage advice, Russell Pellett, Aspex Art Gallery in Portsmouth, my brother 'Gonk' Gorman for his constant support and encouragement and for doing a bang tidy job with proof reading the original manuscript. My multi-talented daughter AJ Gorman for the wonderful cover drawing, Noel Gorman and the rest of my family for their support and patience with all my crazy schemes.

And finally, you dear reader, for purchasing my simple tale.

Contact the Author at: bookdaemon@gmail.com

About the Author

Brendan Thomas Gorman was born in Hackney in the East End of London. He has lived in a number of different towns and cities across southern England and Ireland.

He currently lives in Portsmouth, Hampshire in a massive castle guarded by an army of vicious attack dogs and out-of-work lawyers.

Or he might just be lying and live in a one-bedroomed flat (that's an apartment if you're reading this anywhere outside the United Kingdom).

He is currently single (but informs me that he is open to offers).

The story was written on OpenOffice software (cheers Oracle for the free software!).

Any representations of people alive or dead are purely accidental, honest!

This story may, or may not have actually happened (I'll leave you to decide if you think it's truth, fiction or a mixture of both).

I hope that readers of it will accept it for what I intended it to be when I set out to write it, namely a good fireside tale to tell amongst friends.

The author also feels that this would make a great film and would be happy to discuss this with anyone with lots and lots of money.

WARNING!

This book contains descriptions of torture, murders, explicit sexual acts, drug use, offensive language, blasphemy, general irreverence and reference to British B-list television personalities that some readers may find offensive, or not have heard of.

It also contains a number of clichés and literary clumsiness that some readers may find offensive but hey-ho, what can you do?

If you are easily offended by any of the above I would advise you to stop reading now and give this book to someone who isn't easily offended or too snobbish about the kind of books they read, perhaps as a nice Christmas or birthday present?

For AJ Gorman

you rock my world, dearest daughter

Chapter One

Did you hate Algebra at school? You know the kind of thing: a train leaves London at two pm travelling at an average speed of seventy miles per hour while another train leaves Exeter at midday travelling at an average speed of eighty-five miles per hour...etcetera, etcetera. Boring or what?

I was always more interested in the people on the train and where they were going which is probably why I only got a grade C in my maths exam.

What were the lives of those train passengers like? Were they happy or sad, were they boring or full of excitement? Were they ever likely to meet someone travelling on the other train?

Whenever I travel on a train, I like to imagine stories about my fellow travellers lives.

That man with the green tie and business suit? Not really a businessman at all, lost his job in the city six months ago and spends his working day in the library reading autobiographies of famous explorers.

The thirty-something woman in the Monsoon summer dress with small blue flowers all over it, a teacher in a small provincial primary school? Nope, undercover MI6 agent covertly following the elderly couple opposite her, who the government suspect of selling industrial secrets to the Chinese.

Much more fun than Algebra isn't it?

On a grey Sunday in mid-September a train left London Paddington at two pm heading for the West Country. On this train was a woman in her late twenties, wearing a black cocktail dress and reading a brashly coloured gossip magazine. Half an hour into the journey, she looked up briefly as a train whizzed past in the opposite direction heading into London.

On the other train was a man in his early twenties, sipping at a scalding coffee, watching the houses and embankments speed by.

They didn't see each other and had never met before, but they would meet within the next twelve hours.

This is their story.

Ben glanced around the empty lobby of the Highcliff hotel and sighed heavily. He ran his hands backwards through his spiky ginger hair and looked down at the newspaper on the desk,

Bored, bored, bored...lets see what's on the box tonight? Antiques frigging Roadshow and Songs of bloody Praise...might as well get a DVD out on my way home...

He heard the main front door of the hotel lobby swing open and saw the woman walking towards him. She was wearing a black cocktail dress with sunglasses pushed back onto the top of her hair. She wheeled one of those small luggage cases behind her.

Very nice...quite tasty in fact...late twenties, nice bod...expensive shoes, they look like Jimmy Choo or those Russian sounding ones...bleenies or blenickies or something, he thought, *she looks a bit like that nineteen twenties film star, Louise thingy.*

'Good afternoon, madam...welcome to the Highcliff...how can I be of service?'

'I have a reservation,..Miss Tastyn.'

He looked at the computer screen to his right.

'Ah yes, Miss Tastyn, booked in for a two-week stay until Monday the fifth of October. You requested a balcony room with seaward outlook, you're in room twenty-three...floor four. If I could just see a bank, credit or debit card to confirm your details, I'll get you booked in right away.'

Play it cool, play it cool...this one's hot... Christ, she's a looker, staying alone as well...things are looking up...if I play my cards right...set phasers on stun!

'Could you hurry it up please, I've had quite a long journey from London so I'd like to freshen up and maybe have a nap before dinner.'

Mel thought to herself, *hurry it up you boring jizz-monkey, I'm going to piss myself if you take much longer.*

'Of course, madam, I'll just enter your details and get you to sign our register, then I'll get the porter to show you up.'

Ben pushed a buzzer behind him...*blimey! Calm down darlin'... Keep your knickers on, I'm just trying to do my job here, I'll have to work smoothly with this one.*

'Have you been to Seafordby before? I can highly recommend our bistro bar and sun terrace, fantastic views of the bay...or if you needed some information on bars and clubs in the town perhaps? There are some lively spots in town...although it's starting to wind down a bit after the summer and with the credit crunch, recession and all...you know...ha, ha.'

'Just my room key if that's okay with you, I'll know where to come if I need some information though.'

She handed over a bank card, forced a rapid half smile in his direction, and looked to her right as a door opened, a bent, wizened man with a shock of white hair shuffled rapidly towards her...*shit, he must be all of a hundred years old, I should be helping him upstairs, I just hope he doesn't have a heart attack in the lift!*

'Ah, Ronald, please show this guest up to room twenty-three, if you could just fill in the register for me please. I hope you enjoy your stay with us, and if I can be of service in any way, please don't hesitate to ring down.'

He spun the large register one hundred and eighty degrees with a quick, practised flick of his hand. Mel completed her details and signed the book with a rapid squiggle, thanked Ben, then turned to the weather-beaten old man who was flashing a toothy smile at her.

'Can I help you with your luggage, madam?'

'No...no thanks, I can manage'...Mel smiled at the man.

God, please don't die on me, please don't die on me...just live long enough to get me to my room!

'Very good, madam, please follow me.'

Mel followed the old man, who moved surprisingly quickly despite his obvious ancientness, toward the lift door. They stepped inside and the elderly bell boy pushed the button for the top floor.

'On holiday or is it work?' the bell boy asked.

Mel threw a nervous glance at the man.

'Oh, I guess you could call it a long overdue break.'

She smiled with an air of sadness and looked down awkwardly at her shoes.

'Oh well...yes, I suppose we all need a rest from time to time, God knows I do,' he replied sagely.

Five minutes later Mel stood on the balcony and leaned forward. She bit her bottom lip...hard. She could feel the blood seeping over her teeth and it felt cold and warm and comforting, all at the same time. She could smell the rusty, pungent odour and her brain sent pain signals to tell her to stop what she was doing...because it hurt.

She looked down at large green glass awning covering half of the sun terrace below.

Well, at least I won't feel it when I crash through that roof as I'll already be dead by the time I hit it...two weeks left on this planet...how fucking morbid am I? Shit Mel! Get a grip on yourself, just keep calm and get through it, try to keep it together and enjoy what's left of your life and none of this "woe is me" fuckery!

She puffed her bottom lip out to cool it from the vicious bite, then took in the dramatic view of the bay sweeping up to the headland about a mile away to her right.

She thought about the happy family summer holidays she had spent in this seaside town, and that made her think of her sister Kathy, then she thought of Kathy being dead, fought back the tears and the aching, almost unbearable pain in her chest that always accompanied that thought, and knew that she had to go through with this, that this plan could and would work.

The insurance company will pay out, Kathy can have her treatment, then go back to a normal life with Andy and the kids, I can go out knowing that I did something positive for at least once in my life, it makes everything seem worthwhile, everything makes sense then...fuck.! Keep it together, Mel, it's just two weeks, two weeks partying, a two week bender, major party mayhem for fourteen days, then...it won't matter what happens then.

She wiped hard at her face with the palms of both hands, took some deep breaths to help clear her thoughts which seemed to help her relax, so she went back to surveying the familiar panorama.

Mel turned her head to the left. She could see the crescent shape of the town, spreading out behind the white breakers that crashed onto the pale yellow beach.

The buildings ended abruptly as the ground swept up to the cliffs and headland that marked the northern end of the bay. She could just make out about a dozen or so die-hard surfers bobbing up and down, one or two catching a wave and racing in towards the twinkling lights of the town.

Definitely locals, she thought.

*Only local surf bums would be here at this time of the year, good...that means no poncy city knob jockeys cluttering up the bars and trying to shag anything that's breathing, not that a bit of naughtiness like that might help occupy my mind...*she smiled to herself.

You smutty, dirty girl!!

That's more like the kind of thinking I need!

Mel released her grip on the balcony rail and did a quick one-eighty to face back into the hotel room, she tapped her chin rapidly.

Right! Best foot forward, Melanie.

Shower, glad rags, put some slap on, then time to hit the bar and down a few drinks!

Earlier that day, as Mel was travelling westward on the train, the young man who had been on the train that zipped past in the opposite direction, had arrived in London. He was an employee of the Highcliff Hotel in Seafordby called Will Cummings which is how the two would later meet, but Seafordby was currently a long way from his thoughts.

He stepped into a Soho side-street and pulled the sheet of paper from his back pocket.

These places get more and random, I'm gonna have to find a better way to make some money.

I hope Soho Billy doesn't try another stitch-up like the last wannabe Reggie Cray knob head. If I can finish this up quick I can make it back to Seafordby for my evening shift, and maybe even make it to Sinister Dave's for a late one if it's a quiet night...bonus!!

He studied the instructions on the crumpled A4 sheet and looked out for the sign for "Rita's Pleasure Palace" and spotted a large banana-yellow neon sign that was flashing and fizzing as it spelt out "R...ta's P...easur...P...lace", about three shops down from his position on the pavement.

Yep, must be it, it's definitely tacky enough...mind you I've been in worse places!

He gripped the handles of his eighties original red Gola sports holdall, approached the door immediately to right of the entrance to Rita's and pushed the intercom buzzer,

nothing happened so he pressed it again about a minute later, and then another thirty seconds passed before he heard a gruff, 'yeah...wotcherwant?' He pushed the speak button.

'It's Will from SUBDL'

'OK, mm-commin-dahhnnow...earlimate...wayt-there...'

Will pressed the speak button again,

'Sorry I didn't quite catch...'

There was a static "pop" as the intercom went dead, and he took a step back from the door.

A few minutes later he heard bolts being thrown back and

muttered cursing from the other side of the door. Then as the door swung inwards, Will found himself staring down at what he could only describe a grumpy three-foot-tall body-builder.

'Wheresyerbadge?'

The muscle-bound midget seemed to have the ability to speak without leaving any spaces in his words, which, given that he had one of those voices that sounded like it was the result of smoking sixty cigarettes a day washed down with copious amounts of Napoleon brandy, like a kind of east-end Winston Churchill on speed, made him very difficult to understand.

'Sorry mate? What was that you said? Something about snow white?'

Will grinned cheekily at the vertically challenged roid-monkey.

'Fuggincomedian!...yerbadge...yerbadge!!'

'Ohhh...badge...sorry, here ya go fella.'

Will folded his jacket lapel over to reveal a small gold badge about the size of a fifty-pence piece. It was a perfect golden circle which sported a raised silver motif of two crossed darts with the embossed initials, *SUBDL* in a semi-circle around the bottom of the badge.

The mini-doorman, grunted and made a "come on in" gesture by flicking his head towards his left shoulder.

Will walked past the doorman and waited in the narrow hallway as the man pushed the heavy wooden door closed, then reached behind the door for a stool which he positioned at the bottom of the door, and then stood on in order to reach the top deadbolts.

When he had finished securing the door, he walked past Will without a glance and stood at the bottom of the stairs...

'Follame-funniman'

Will shook his head in disbelief and followed the man up the stairs.

It was surprisingly clean if a little gloomy, but tackily

decorated, or so Will thought. They went up four flights of stairs, past long corridors on each floor that lead towards the rear of the building. Will could hear the moans of couples mid-shag and tried to block them out to focus on the imminent game. The smell of stale sweat and semen mixed with industrial disinfectant was more difficult to block out.

He had watched a couple of DVDs of Terry's games before and had noticed a few weaknesses in his opponents play, mainly that he sometimes seemed to miss crucial check-outs when he was under pressure and seemed to be showing symptoms of what most dart players referred to as "the Yips". An uncontrollable shaking of the throwing hand. This would mean that most of the sensible money would go on Will as one of the rising stars of SUBDL

This was only his second match of the year and he knew that at most, if he was lucky and he won, he would only get two more matches this year, the southern regional final and then the national final and glory!

He thought back to when he had first come across the *Social Underclass of Britain Darts League.* It was six years ago and he'd been serving three years in Pentonville for a class A drug offence. Namely that he'd been caught with eighty ecstasy tablets outside a house in North London and despite his protestations that they were mainly for personal use, the police were coming down hard at that time on "disco-biscuit peddlin' scrote's" as the Drug Squad detective who had collared Will had referred to him.

In reality, the police were after the bigger fish at the top end of the food chain and when Will couldn't give them any names because he genuinely didn't know any, they just plain refused to believe him and threw the book at him…well…there was also the fact that he had called the detective sergeant a "potato-headed pig-fondler" without knowing that the DS's nickname at the station was "Mr Potato-Head" due to his uncanny resemblance to the popular children's toy of the same name.

The DS knew about the nickname and hated it, but refused to shave off his moustache and lose a few stone (which would have at least given pause to his workmates, although once a station nickname stuck it generally stayed stuck).

This was mainly out of pure...pig-headedness basically, so Will's comment, whilst humorous and somewhat accurate, also sealed his fate as the DS made a personal point of ensuring that Will did a stretch in prison.

So when after a couple of months inside, as a frightened twenty-one-year-old "first timer", a guy called Luke Murphy approached Will after watching him play a darts match against a fellow inmate and asked him if he was interested in making some money out of competitive darts.

Will thought he was joking. He was surprised to see a dart board in the games room and had expressed this to Luke when he first arrived.

Luke simply pointed at the pool table and said, 'What's that?'

Will had looked at him to see if he was winding him up, 'Erm...a pool table?'

Luke smiled at Will.

'Top marks bright boy, now what do you think would happen if that big bruiser about to pot the eight ball took offence to his mucker there coughing as he was about to play his shot, snapped his cue in half and jabbed the jagged end in the other guys neck eh?'

'Err, he'd be in a lot of trouble and the screws would take away the pool table?'

Luke patted Will on the head. 'Spot on fresh-meat! As well as that, 'e would 'ave the rest of his brethren to answer to, and as you can imagine, 'aving seventy odd nut-cases wanting to see you strung up by your crown jewels, does not improve your chances of survival in this gaff! So tell me bruvver, wot would you rather 'ave jabbed in your neck, the broken end of a pool cue or a poxy little dart?'

9

Will nodded and smiled at Luke.

'Good point.'

He'd played County League level darts as a teenager but given up at eighteen when he discovered there was a world of other fun stuff outside of throwing arrows, stuff like drugs, drink and girls.

He found out rapidly that the darts league involved some heavy gambling on matches that ran into tens of thousands of pounds and it was far from a joke.

The rules of SUBDL were very strictly adhered to and breaches (when they did rarely occur) would be guaranteed to result in broken hands and fingers amputated. All League players must have served or be serving "real time" of over six months and were not to have played at anything above County level. This was to ensure a relatively level playing field and a high number of upsets. Also betting was tightly controlled within the membership and players received a fixed amount for each match of a grand plus a win bonus of a grand once they graduated to the "outside league" when they got to the end of their prison stay.

Any player caught laying off bets or attempting to throw games or having a history of playing at a higher level would be subjected to the standard hand-mutilating punishments already mentioned. Nobody talked about what happened if someone grassed to the screws about the league, but it was generally accepted that the punishments would be pretty horrific for such a major transgression. This ensured that what happened in SUBDL stayed in SUBDL

A bit like "Fight Club" really.

Except without the...erm...bare-knuckle boxing, the blowing up buildings, soap manufacturing and IKEA furniture.

When Will was released after eighteen months, he was automatically entered into the Outside League which followed the same rules as before, but games were broadcast live on the internet to allow for online betting. Today would be a big game as Will had climbed to number three in the Southern Area rankings, Terry "The Tornado" Matthews was number two, so this was the Regional semi-final.

*Fuckin Tornado, more like "mild breeze Matthews" this twat ought to be called...*thought Will, puffing as he reached the top of the fourth flight of stairs.

The midget doorman led him along a short corridor, opened a door at the end and they entered a large plush oak-panelled office with an old-fashioned and expensive-looking desk immediately opposite them.

Sat behind this desk in a black leather armchair that looked three sizes too big for him was Soho Billy. Shoulder-length greasy black hair, cheesy goatee beard, mad staring eyes and five foot four of wiry muscle.

'Will, you carrot-crunching wankah! How the fuck are you, fellah?'

'Not three-bad, Billy, how's you? Business is good by the sound of many beasts with two backs on the way up the stairs.'

'Haw-haw! Nice one Will, you always were an unfunny little shit! Anyway, good to see you my boy, I see you've met Eddie my assistant, you'll have to excuse his foul mood, I forgot to feed him this morning, that and the fact that he has a nasty case of crabs that he caught off one of my girls, haw-haw!'

Eddie the Doorman just scowled and muttered a short sentence which sounded like 'Dint-no-tart-wus-durtibitch,' and scratched his crotch frantically as though to hammer home his personal anguish.

Will had met Soho Billy at a couple of games last year when Billy was acting as the Match Official League Invigilator or "mollie" as the players called them.

All the remaining games for this season were due to be played at this venue so he would be seeing a lot more of Billy over the next couple of weeks.

Will thought he was a sleazy porn merchant and pimp with issues about the fact he was only just over five-feet tall, which explained the midget henchman. *Makes him feel superior I suppose,* Will reasoned.

His dubious business concerns and personality aside, he was known as a fair referee and Will was happy that Billy was someone he knew would play it by the book.

'Right then, enough of the chit-chat, let's get on with the business in hand shall we?

Tornado ain't here yet so we'll go on through and you can check out the oche and all that guff, follow me, West Coast!'

Will didn't care much for the obsession with nicknames and acronyms that populated this twilight pseudo-sporting world, but he supposed it could have been worse. *I could have ended up as Will "the Whirlwind" or "the Whippet" Cummings...fuck that! I'm glad it's only "West Coast"!*

Billy led Will through a door behind the desk and into a large high-ceilinged room with a polished wooden floor. There were about twenty blokes, about half that number of women sitting around the room at wooden tables with glasses of dark brown or golden liquid, half full ashtrays arrayed on the cheap plastic red and white checker-board tablecloths.

A stereotypical busty barmaid filed her nails behind the bar and pretended not to be listening to the three fat "security" types who propped up the bar, nudging and giggling to each other like adolescent schoolboys as they made lewd, sexual comments and tried to provoke a reaction from her.

A massive bearded biker-type wearing an old Hawkwind T-shirt that displayed his multitude of tattoos to their best, sat behind a table at one side of the room with a tripod-mounted camera and laptop positioned on the table itself. At the far end of the room was a large raised dais, lit up by an overpowering lighting rig with three green baize covered walls forming a half-hexagon on one side of the structure. A Winnmau championship standard board was fixed to the central wall with an electronic scoreboard to the left of the board.

The air was thick with cigarette and cigar smoke and the smell of stale perfume and after shave. A few nods of recognition were thrown at Will from blokes he recognised from Pentonville and previous meets. He returned them politely but was trying to get his game face on.

Not quite Lakeside, but legitimate enough and that would do for Will.

He smiled and placed the sports holdall down and looked around the room like a boxer surveying the crowd before a title fight, nodding in approval and confident of victory. *Let's get ready to go postal on the Tornado's arse!*

He was tight in the first set, as most of the crowd were supporting the Tornado who had marched onto the stage to whoops and cheers as The Prodigy's *Smack my bitch up* boomed around the hall.

He had come on to Tony de Vit's *The Dawn* to a much more reserved welcome. Soho Billy announced that as it was the semi-final it would be the best of nine sets.

In other words, a bloody marathon! thought Will.

The arrows were poor in the opening set and he lost the throw quickly, followed by the set at a score of three-two.

He quickly re-focused and won the second set closely, followed by winning the third set very luckily, with the Tornado suffering a series of bounce outs and hitting the wrong side of the wire when he had easy doubles to go at. More importantly, Will had first quietened the crowd, then won them over as the match went on. They shared the next two sets with Tornado improving in the sixth set. Will was now four-two up with a potential three sets remaining.

After forty-five minutes of play, Will wiped the beads of perspiration from his face with several slow, deliberate swipes of his forearm, cupping the darts lovingly in the palm of his left hand. He could feel his heart pumping at an incredible rate in his chest, his throwing arm muscles ached with the lactic acid build up and he could hear the swooshing heavy bass soundtrack of blood pulsing through his head. He glanced around and saw the look of defeat in Terry's expression. Tornado had just missed his chance to stay in the game with two darts at double sixteen.

He had bottled it and left Will with a check-out of forty-five.

Soho Billy announced this over the microphone and Will turned back to the board. He relaxed and released his first arrow into the heart of the single thirteen. He only needed one arrow to hit the centre of double sixteen

'Yeeesss!!'...Will punched the air and gave a small leap. The crowd cheered and clapped their approval.

Soho Billy stepped forward and announced loudly

'Game, set, and the match, to Will "West-Coast" Cummins! Five sets to two!'

Will got changed into his uniform quickly, he headed down the back stairs and through the empty and now eerily quiet hotel kitchen. It was an hour after the last meal service and Will knew it must have been a slow night, as the chef and his staff had already cleared up and left for the evening. The only noise was the constant electrical buzzing of the large bug-zappers and industrial-sized fridges. He had finished the game in London early enough to get to the bank, deposit his two grand match money and call in to see Luke, his old mate from Pentonville. Luke had been in good form and had pushed a fat envelope into Wills inside jacket pocket as they parted which contained "sumfink for the weekend, bro" as Luke had cheerily explained. He had checked the envelope as soon as he was out of Luke's sight, inside were seven small blue triangular ecstasy tablets in a clear plastic baggie, and a much larger bag of weed, he smiled to himself,

Eccy's and skunk, nice one, Luke!

As he walked to the door and into the bar storage area, he could hear the soft jazz/elevator muzak from the main bar area beyond. Crossing the storage area, being careful to avoid the beer barrels and crates, he peered through the porthole window of the door to the room beyond. Will could see the three customers scattered around the bar. An elderly couple dressed sharpish for dinner and nursing their after dinner cocktails, but his eyes were almost immediately drawn to a dark-haired girl sat alone, playing with the ice in her drink and staring vacantly into space. She reminded him of someone famous. *An actress*?

He took in the laughter lines starting to develop around her pale blue eyes and the darkness of her ink black hair, both ends of her short French bob sweeping forwards to point at her high cheekbones like black arrows.

He jumped back suddenly as Mike, his working partner for that evening, squashed his face hard against the glass porthole, let out a low gurgling moan and raised his middle finger slowly up to the glass. 'Ass hole' mouthed Will silently.

He saw Mike's face break into a leering grin and watched as Mike then dribbled some saliva down the glass, moved his face away and started laughing. Will pushed quickly through the swing door causing Mike to leap back dramatically.

'Whoaa!...easy there tiger, wot time do ya call this?'

Mike's faux over-reaction made Will smile.

'Sorry mate, train from the Smoke took fucking ages, besides, I'm only an hour late and I can see it's not exactly Friday night at The Ministry of Sound is it?'

They were careful to keep their conversation low so that the customers wouldn't be able to hear. As they knew from previous complaints and written warnings from management, it was important that guests were not able to eavesdrop. The cheesy easy-listening bar soundtrack also helped muffle their conversation.

'I take it you managed to sneak past our eagle-eyed jean-jeur officer of the laur?'

Will laughed at Mike's half decent attempt at an Inspector Clouseau impersonation.

'Yeah, he hasn't been in here has he?'

'Nah, mate, too busy tugging off over his Seven of Nine calendar'

Will sniggered again.

Ben the receptionist, or "Duty Manager" as he liked to call himself, was a rabid Trekkie and a huge Jeri Ryan fan. Will and Mike had ribbed him mercilessly when all the allegations of her attending wild sex parties with her dodgy politician ex-husband were splashed all over the media. So any mention by anyone of the "Seven of Nine" title referring to the number of blokes she used to pick out and then shag at said parties would send Ben into a fit of apoplexy.

Will glanced over Mike's shoulder at the dark-haired girl again,

'Aha! So you've spotted our hot new arrival, well back off, buddy! I saw her first so I get first crack at her, once Mister and Missus Bus Pass finish their cocktails.'

Mike flicked his index fingers at Will's shoulders and grinned mischievously as he said this. Will gave a Gallic shrug and turned his palms upwards.

'Fair enough, mate, but I've got a tenner says she blows you out in under five minutes.'

Mike smiled and offered his hand to Will.

'You are so on, dude!'

As if on cue, the couple raised themselves stiffly from the plush sofa and said goodnight to Mel and then to Will and Mike.

Mike swept both hands through his surf-and-sun-bleached blond locks and turned to Will.

'Prepare to watch a master at work and recognise my total awesomeness fella!'

Will made a low bow with an "after you" gesture with his

hand towards the end of the counter and then picked up a glass and started to polish it slowly and deliberately, glancing at the girl every now and again to check if she was reacting to Mike in any discernible way.

Mike went to the table where the couple had been sitting first to collect the empty glasses, he veered smoothly towards Mel's table as he returned and perched himself on the end of the leather sofa. She smiled sweetly at him.

'Hi, is everything okay? Anything else I can get you?'

Mike gave her his best surf-boy smile to reveal a perfect set of white teeth that were enhanced by his tan and almost white-blond curly hair. This was the smile that had been known to cause girls to melt like ice-cream on a hot July day, or so he claimed.

'I'm fine at the moment, but thanks for asking,'

replied Mel.

Mike rested the two glasses on one leg, using his free arm to support himself as he leaned in closer towards her.

'Listen, this place is dead, I can get off in a hour at nine and I was wondering if I might show you around, there's a couple of good pubs and clubs in town...so...how's that sound? It'll be a lot more fun than this place.'

Mel smiled again and flicked her hair.

'Thanks for your offer, but I'd rather your friend over there escorted me.'

Mike made a disgusted face like he'd stepped in something nasty.

'What, Will? Wasting your time there darlin', he's a friend of Dorothy.'

'Really?' replied Mel with fake surprise, glancing over at Will.

'He doesn't look like he travels on the other bus?'

'Oh yeah, he's a fully-paid-up member of the uphill gardeners club, huge fan of musical theatre and interior design'

Mel stared hard at the grinning Mike.

'He's not really gay is he? You're just making all this up aren't you?

As well as being a bit over the top on the homophobic remarks. You sure you're not trying to cover up for a slight desire to go over the rainbow yourself?'

Mike was still thrown from the almost instant rejection of what he regarded as his surefire never-fail, earthy charms, and now he was slightly panicked by the worry that he might have subconscious homosexual leanings.

He was not used to knock-backs as he normally had plenty of attention, due to the fact that he looked as he'd just walked off the set of a sixties surfer B-movie.

'Erm, oh crap! Yeah, okay. He's not really gay but I'm much more fun, honest, and besides he's got no hair, well hardly any.'

'Mmmm!' Mel purred.

'I've always liked the gangly skinhead look and sorry, you're really nice and all that but I don't really go for surfer types.'

She gave a little shrug and reached quickly for her drink.

By this stage Mike realised that she had already made her mind up so he smiled and winked at Mel.

'Well, okay, can't blame a guy for trying eh? He is actually a really nice bloke, and a good mate as well, I'll send him over.'

Mike stood up and gave a low dramatic bow with his arms outstretched, still holding the empty glasses in one hand. He retreated to the bar and smiled at Will who had been watching the scene carefully but was unable to hear how it had gone.

'Well?' He examined Mike's face for some hint of success or failure.

Mike grinned widely and lent forward to whisper quietly,

'I owe you a tenner mate, oh and by the way,

she wants to talk to you, you jammy git!

I tried to tell her that you prefer gentlemen's bottoms but she rumbled that one straight away!'

'What? You have got to be kidding, she wants to talk to me?'

Will looked doubtfully at Mike, trying to work out if he was winding him up.

'See for yourself, mate.'

Mike jerked a thumb towards his shoulder and when Will looked over at Mel she smiled coyly and gave him a nervous little wave.

Will looked back at Mike and broke into a huge smile.

'See! Told ya, although what she sees in a bald-headed, skinny runt like you I don't know!'

Mike looked grumpy and defeated.

'Now, now…toys back in the pram, bad losers and all that. I don't suppose?'

Will looked hopefully at Mike.

'Yeah...I'll cover for you in case the ginger whinger comes snooping, but you better go and ask him if he wants a lemonade or is it Klingon blood wine he drinks now? Otherwise he won't believe you've been in at all tonight.'

'Cheers, mate, you're flippin' golden, I bloody luv you!'

Will made a grab for Mike who quickly backed away and raised his arms to fend off Will.

'Yeah, yeah, I know, enough of that or she really will think you stroll up Bourneville Boulevard. Be off with you!'

Will winked at Mike then made his way from behind the bar to where Mel was sitting,

'Erm… Hi, I'm Will…'

'Yes, I know, the "Big Wednesday" extra over there told me.'

Mel smiled and nodded towards Mike.

'I'm Mel'

'Nice to meet you, Mel, can I get you another drink?'

'Why the hell not, double voddy & coke please, and I hear you might be giving me a guided tour of Seafordby later?'

Mel put on her best innocent little girl look and watched for Will's reaction. She had spotted him as soon as he came through the back door to the bar, quick and sort of graceful but with jerky, rapid hand movements that made him look clumsy, awkward and cool, all at the same time.

'Blimey, you don't hang around you? Are you always this forward?'

Will smiled and admitted to himself that she was the most stunning-looking woman he could ever remember seeing, she had him hooked from the moment he saw her from the bar storage room.

'Hanging around is for wimps and losers, honey,

and I'm on holiday from wimps and losers, now do I get my drink or not Will?'

Mel waved her empty glass at Will and giggled.

Will stood up quickly, took the empty with a quick sweep of his arm and gave a quick nod of his head.

'Mel my sweet, it will be my great pleasure and privilege to bring your drink, and in one hour's time to escort you on a personal tour of the wondrous delights of our fair seaside paradise.'

'Ooh la-la! How can a young lady resist such a generous offer from so gallant a knight! Are you sure you're not a little bit of a bum-boy? I mean, coming out with all that flowery crap?'

Mel laughed heartily and Will joined in with her.

'No, I prefer ladies, and very beautiful ladies always inspire the poet in me, I'll fetch that drink for you right away!'

'Smoothie,'

said Mel, checking out Wills rear as he headed back to the bar.

'Why, thank you,' Will replied over his shoulder.

An hour later Will escorted Mel quietly out of the staff entrance, and they set off down the hill towards the town centre.

They could see the glitzy but gaudy neon lights from the amusement park, hear the screams of excitement and cheers of revellers drifting up on the clear September night breeze.

'Right then, Sir William, where do we hit first?'

Mel did a small curtsey and smiled at Will.

'Well, I thought we could go to Sinister Dave's place.'

Mel linked both her arms through Will's arm.

'Woohhh!....Sinister Dave! He sounds really scary!'

Mel rolled her eyes for extra dramatic effect.

'Not really,' said Will.

'He's as camp as Christmas, everyone used to call him "big fat gay Dave" but he didn't think that held enough cachet for a nightclub owner, and it's a bit of a long nickname. Then his Italian boyfriend, Guido noticed he was left-handed and told him that the Latin for left-handed was "Sinestre" so he became "Sinister Dave"! Wait until you meet him, he's about as sinister as a Battenburg sponge cake.'

Mel snorted a laugh.

'Jeez, you lot are bloody weird down here, must be all the sea air, ketamine and crack cocaine.'

Will laughed.

'I wouldn't know about that, the weirdness down here is more likely the result of it being a little bit of a forgotten seaside town, but speaking of illegal substances.'

Will reached into his jeans pocket and then held out small two triangular blue pills in palm, he grinned at Mel.

'I thought these might get the evening going on the right track.'

Mel let out a little cry of delight.

'Whoo! Eccy's! And they look like Blue Meanies to me? Cheers, me dear, don't mind if I do!'

Mel reached into Will's open palm and quickly popped the pill into her mouth. Will did the same and Mel hugged into Will's arm more closely as they continued down the hill.

She had noticed Will as soon as came into the bar, had pretended to ignore his knockabout antics with the other barman but felt drawn to him, a very definite and clear physical attraction. She liked his sparkling green eyes, and that he seemed to have a kind of quiet sadness in his expression, like he also had some kind of deep, hurtful secret that he was unable to tell anyone about.

He's like me...damaged goods,
she had thought to herself.

Mel stopped suddenly which brought Will to an immediate halt and turned to face him. 'I know you already think I'm a fast mover but do you mind if I kiss you now, I mean before this pill takes effect, I mean I know it might be starting to work already but, you know, I want it to be...more natural?'

Mel looked nervously at Will.

Will looked deeply into her eyes and smiled.

'I'd like that... I'd like that a lot.'

They leaned forward and held each other closer and closer until their lips met. Their mouths opened slightly and the kiss began.

Mel was right as the MDMA had already started its work on the brain's pleasure centres, and this heightened the sensation for both of them.

Mel thought a bomb had gone off in the pit of stomach. She felt dizzy and heat began to spread from the base of her spine and she thought she was going to melt, or explode or both. She could feel her heart pounding and she could feel Wills heart pounding back against her chest, like they were two prisoners in neighbouring cells, knocking on the walls trying to communicate desperately with each other.

Will felt like he had stood on a live electric cable, he tingled all over and could feel his cock trying to grow and escape from his boxer shorts. The hair stood up on the back of his neck and he felt dizzy, light-headed and euphoric. He could feel his heart pounding against Mel's, like, well...like two prisoners in neighbouring cells, knocking on the walls trying to communicate desperately with other.

In other words, it was awesome.

After a while, the kiss ended and they moved apart slightly.

'Shit! That was really bloody great,'

said Will.

'It kinda was wasn't it?' Mel replied.

There was a long pause where they just held each other and enjoyed the moment.

'Come on,'

said Mel, 'we've got some partying to do!'

She grabbed Will's hand and they ran, laughing like drains, down the hill and into the waiting town below.

Chapter Two

Kelly had been watching the house for two days. She had slipped over the fence at 6.30 am when she knew that this would give her at least an hour to get in position, set up and be ready to go.

She flexed her muscles in turn to ward off the creeping stiffness and checked her watch.

7.30, he'll be getting up soon, I'd better do final check.

She thought of her dad and could hear his deep Norfolk twang echo around in her mind...*measure twice and then cut Kelly, that way, you can be sure to get just the right length.*

She knew that Judge Gordon Edwards was a creature of habit, he would come into the garden between 7.45 and 8.00 am, stretch, yawn, then sit down at the table and read his paper and drink his cup of Darjeeling, unless it was raining, as it had been the first day and he had sat in the conservatory.

No good to me in there, he has to be outside!

She had found out about his affair and his secret Cotswold hideaway from Barnaby, her handler.

I suppose as a Criminal Lawyer he would know who High Court Judge Edwards was shagging, the dirty old bugger...I wonder if his wife is paying for this hit?

From watching the house, Kelly knew that the girlfriend, twenty-two-year-old page-three stunner Louise, didn't get out of bed till mid-day so there was every chance that the judge's body wouldn't be discovered for over three hours.

She checked her modified Telinject Vario 3V dart rifle again and pulled the Velcro pocket open on the side of her black hold-all. She took out the small box and opened it to check the three bio-bullets were still intact. They were modified to be half the size of a normal bio-bullet used for deer inoculation and were one centimetre long by 0.37 centimetres in diameter, tiny but deadly.

Especially as she had loaded the bullets with a 125mg dose of poison.

In fact the poison had been the most difficult and expensive thing to get hold of. She had spent ten thousand of her fifty-thousand-pound fee getting the *Phyllobates Terribilis* poison shipped from Columbia via Ecuador and then Jamaica. The 'Poison Dart Frog' venom had to be collected from frogs captured in the wild as captive bred frogs would not produce the right toxicity due to diet, and her research had told her that one milligram of the poison was enough to kill eight people.

She also knew, from testing a few "un-modified" bio-bullets on herself that, by adjusting the psi pressure on the rifle, the bullet left a tiny wound, a bit like a bad insect bite, with some bruising which faded after about an hour (she had remote fired the rifle at her chest from 50 meters, repeatedly until she got the penetration just right).

And the bullet itself would dissolve to leave a small intramuscular residue.

Measure twice, and then cut. Dad again!

If she could make her favoured shot, *if he's facing me when he yawns*, she knew that the pathologist would find the poison in the judge's blood toxicology report on *post-mortem* examination, but would struggle to work out how it got there until he checked inside the back of the judge's mouth. She liked making life difficult for the authorities. It was her way of paying them back for making her teenage years so difficult when she had been taken into care at fourteen.

Kelly could still remember vividly the night when the police had knocked on the door of the cottage she shared with her father to break the news that he wasn't coming home ever again, had blamed them for turning her into the tortured and confused individual she worked so hard to escape from.

Kelly heard the buzzing of the alarm from the bedroom, then

it stopped suddenly and she heard the judge coughing.

*Time to get this show on the road...*she hummed Dizzie Rascal's song *Bonkers* lightly under her breath and reached over, opening the small black box and revealed the three tiny bio-bullets, sitting in their tiny black felt coffins and looking more like broken tips of a child's crayon than lethal vehicles of death.

She then undid a zip on the top breast pocket of her camouflage jacket and took out a small magazine and pair of plastic tweezers. Hands moving skilfully and quickly, Kelly loaded the bio-bullets into the magazine using the tweezers to gently but firmly locate each dart in place and then locked the magazine into its housing on the rifle.

She shifted back into a position so that she was kneeling on one knee, with her elbow supported by the other knee, put the tweezers back into her jacket and brought the rifle up to her shoulder.

Her carefully chosen spot was halfway down the garden about 30 meters away from the conservatory and rear decking area and was well hidden deep in the large evergreen bush.

It was a quiet morning and she could hear the judge clattering about in the kitchen above the sound of birdsong and other wildlife.

Kelly let her mind wander for five minutes, she knew that she had at least ten minutes before the judge would make an appearance.

Wonder what the twins are having for lunch? I'll have to phone as soon as I finish here, I should catch them before playgroup. Picnic this weekend if the weather's nice.

I might even take them to Longleat, they love the lions so much bless 'em! Anyway, back to work, Kelly girl!

She moved her head back to the telescopic site of the rifle and started her breathing routine, senses snapping back into focus as she smelt different animals on the wind. Fox, cat, along with the rank stink of a hedgehog filled her nostrils.

She was at home again, she felt comfortable, like those nights spent with her dad on the estate, tracking down the poachers and keeping the animals safe. She could still remember the smell of her father when he crouched up close, right next to her, the pungent odour of tobacco and linseed oil mixed with earth, coming off his enormous Barbour jacket.

The conservatory door creaked open and Judge Edwards stepped out onto the expensive pine decking. He placed his newspaper, then his cup of tea on the patio table and looked out proudly on his "hideaway paradise". Life was good, he was rich, he was happy, he had a wife, a mistress and two children at Oxford, all of those aspirational goals set by his parents and his ancestry had been achieved, he felt good.

Kelly felt her muscles tense as she focused on her target area.

Come on...come on...open that rancid gob of yours!

He raised his arms and stretched them wide above his head and began a long yawn, suddenly he felt a sting at the back of his throat, like a bee had flown in and stung him. Then he felt an intense pain and it was as though everything had gone into slow motion. He threw his fingers into his mouth to try to pull out the sting but he felt faint and was about to vomit, so used his other hand to steady himself on the table.

*I'd better sit down, I feel sick...*was the last thought that went through his mind.

Kelly watched as the judge tried desperately to reach into his mouth to extract the poison dart, then he suddenly lurched forwards and fell flat on his face, his body making a load bang as it impacted with the hard wooden deck.

She listened for sounds of activity from the house but all she could hear was birdsong and other wildlife.

Good, Louise didn't hear tha , she won't be up for ages yet, the lazy cow.

She packed her dart rifle in the long black holdall and slung it silently over her shoulder. Edging backwards slowly out of the large bush she checked and covered her tracks and signs that somebody had been concealed in there. Moving around the bush and onto the lawn of the garden, her senses went into overdrive and adrenalin pumping as she approached the judge's body and knelt down next to him, using a felt- gloved hand to check his neck for a pulse.

It was there, but very, very weak.

Kelly swung her leg back and kicked the judge hard, right in the balls. 'Take that you fuck-pig!'

There was no reaction from the prone figure.

I'd give you about five minutes at most Judge Edwards, which is more time than you gave to that rapist last year, what did you say about the victim?... "The reliability and integrity of the main prosecution witness causes me to have some serious doubts about her testimony, which I would like the members of the jury to consider when deliberating, namely that she has changed her statement on more than one occasion and how we have heard other evidence of her lifestyle and social interactions."

What you meant was that because she's a single mum she must have been gagging for it! You low-life piece of shit!

How ironic then, that you've been taken out by a single mum from a North London sink-estate then you hypocritical fucktard!

Kelly backed away quietly from the judge then turned and walked to the end of the garden. Ten minutes later as she was making her way through the woods, she felt a buzzing vibration on the outside of her left thigh.

She reached down and undid the Velcro pocket on her black catsuit and pulled out the mobile phone.

'Mornin', Barnaby.'

'Good morning, my dear, I take it our esteemed friend has met his untimely but nonetheless deserved end?'

'Fuck sake, Barnaby! Why do you always have to talk like you're in some Agatha Christie TV drama? If you mean, is he dead then yes, and I reckon it'll be a while before he's found as well. Sleeping Implants ain't gonna wake up for ages yet, but I want to get back to my girls, so hurry it up, mate!'

'Apologies, my dear, please forgive my penchant for the more melodramatic turn of phrase, you know how I've always had such a deep and abiding love for the pure theatrical wickedness of our little enterprise, you like cavorting in the forest playing at ninjas, I prefer a good P.G. Woodhouse and a cheeky little Montrachet, we all have our foibles, indulge me dearest.'

Kelly thought that Barnaby always overdid his "theatrical luvvie" act, in that he did sound a bit like Olivier or Geilgud with his received pronunciation and dramatic verbal diarrhoea, but given the fact he was about twenty stone, five and half feet tall with curly grey hair and a shaggy beard and so looked more like that doctor from *Holby City*, it just didn't sound to her like his voice fitted his body.

'Get to the sodding point, Barnaby, what's the job this time?'

'You cut me to the quick darling, you know how my heart skips a beat whenever I hear your dulcet tones, nevertheless I appreciate that time is money...etcetera, etcetera. How would you fancy a little trip to the seaside next Sunday week? The West Country is so lovely this time of year.'

'Sounds fab, how much?'

Kelly pulled at the elastic hair-band holding her bleached blonde curls in a tight ponytail and shook them free as she effort-lessly jogged through the woodland. She had parked her car up a dirt track in a fairly isolated and remote wooded valley, about fifteen minutes speed-walk from the judge's country shag-pad.

'An easy sixteen-K dearest darling, normally I wouldn't trouble you with such a Lilliputian endeavour but I took the liberty of assuming you'd prefer something less ...ahem, Machiavellian for your next task, a departure from the intensity of your current enterprise. It's a quick in and out job, a mere trifle, I've left the details in the usual dead-drop. You can have a quick look-see and let me know if you're interested later today hmm?'

'I'll 'ave to check if Darren can look after the girls, I'll get back to you later, bye Barnaby.'

Kelly clicked the mobile shut and slid it back into the leg pocket. She quickened her pace and thought about the girls.

Wonder what mischief they're getting up to…Destiny and Harmony, my little angels!

Kelly's children had been given their names by Darren, Kelly's ex-husband. A huge Gerry Anderson fan, he had hoped for triplets so he could call the third one "Rhapsody" and he would have the full set of Captain Scarlet's "Angels".

Kelly had found his childlike outlook on the world endearing when they had first met, but when she realised after two years of marriage that his childishness extended to a full blown refusal to take responsibility for any aspect of their lives, she got shot of him as soon as she could.

They had a much better relationship now and despite his failings as an adult, his inherent good nature, cheerfulness and juvenile demeanour meant that he was great with the twins and they adored their dad in the way that many daughters do.

She arrived at the back of her silver Audi RS Spyder convertible and changed quickly into her business suit, applied some scarlet-flame red lippy, long-lash mascara and popped on her Gucci sunglasses. She swung into the driver's seat and started the engine, pausing briefly to run a brush through, then check her hair in the mirror as the Blaupunt kicked into life and the Sugababes' *About you now* blasted around the car.

Kelly turned on the iPhone in its dashboard mounting and hooked the Bluetooth headset around her ear and jabbed her fingers at the screen.

'Hello, Harmony babes, are you having fun with Daddy?… Awww, Mummy loves you too, precious, go and get your sister so I can say hello to her before play school!'

Ten minutes later, looking for all the world like a wealthy Cotswold princess, well either that or a very successful hairdresser, she pulled out of the forest dirt track and onto the tarmac of the quiet Gloucestershire B-road, humming along to the tunes blasting from the car stereo.

'Lucy?... Hello, sweetness, having a nice time?.... Is Jasmine with you? Good... what?... Yes, yes, darling, listen, it's ten o'clock and there are only fifty people in here petal, now I know your poor little tootsies are vewy, vewy sore from the killer Jimmy Choo's I bought you, but I'd appreciate it if you two could get off your perfectly formed, if way too skinny, white arses and wriggle around a few pubs and drum up some customers for your uber-glam Uncle Dave, rather than sitting in The Red Lion and flashing your breasticles at your gorgeous and divine, but equally useless boyfriends, otherwise what's the point of me paying you my little flowers?

What?...good girls,...speak to you later...byeee! Me love you long time!...byeee!

Sweet Lady Ga-Ga!... What a pair of useless spunk-buckets... Guido, angel-heart, be a love and make me one of your fab double strength Martini's before I explode with frustration!!... Thank you, precious!'

Dave cast a weary eye around his *Blue Lagoon Nite Club* empire, sighed, then mopped his damp forehead with a pristine red silk handkerchief pulled from the top pocket of his two-tone designer smoking jacket.

Oh well, another season nearly over, time to start planning for the hols, maybe I'll take Guido to Mauritius this winter? Goa was just too much like an Pan-Asian Ibiza last year...or maybe we could try South America?

Dave watched as Mel and Will tumbled into the club, laughing and hugging, their pupils the size of chocolate buttons.

Awww!,to be young and in love! How sweet.

'Coo-ee! Will! Over here sweetheart!'

Will grabbed Mel by the hand and turned to face her grinning, 'Come on, babe, you've got to meet Dave, he's a riot!'

Mel smiled back at Will and examined his face, suddenly her expression changed to a one of slight panic.

'Shit man! You're pupils are massive! Are mine? Ohh shit! He'll notice, do you think he'll notice? He wont kick us out will he? The music's great in here! Fuck these are good pills, I'm off me tits! Hee, hee, hee!... Fuck, my heart's racing, I'm sooo off me face!'.

Will laughed as Mel machine-gunned the questions at him like five-year-old that's had an overdose of Haribo.

'It's ok, Mel, Dave's cool about pills as long as you're not blatantly taking them and you're not out of control, and if you don't deal in the club toilets, he's not daft but he knows people do it, it's a night club after all and yes, these are good pills and I've just come up on mine and fuck! I've just realised I'm talking faster than you and most of it's crap so let's go talk to him!'

They both laughed and moved over to Dave.

Dave grabbed Will dramatically by the shoulders then leant in and 'air kissed' him.

'Will my darling boy, it's been too long you wicked, wicked child! You know I get withdrawal symptoms if I don't get a dose of Willy regularly!'

All three of them started laughing uncontrollably at this.

'And just who is this gorgeous creature on your arm? Why, it's either Louise Brooks re-incarnated or Aphrodite herself has decided to come down from Mount Olympus to play with the hearts of mortals once again hmm?'

Mel giggled at this and gave a little theatrical curtsey.

Will was still laughing.

'Dave, this is Mel, Mel meet Sinister Dave.'

Mel offered a hand which Dave took in his and then bowed to

kiss her knuckles.

'Oh, great goddess of ancient Greece! You humble us mortals with your presence and dazzle us with your beauty, now show us your tits! Ha ha ha ha!'

'Stop it!' Mel laughed. 'You're wicked! And you if you keep this up I'll wet myself!'

'As you command, O Queen! Besides, I don't want urine all over me nice new shag-pile now do I? By the way, you two, I couldn't help noticing that you're pupils are the size of dinner plates, I take it you're in the sweet embrace of the love drug?'

Will grinned sheepishly at Dave.

'Uhh, yeah is that okay, Dave?'

'Of course, dumpling, as long as you can handle it and don't throw a "whitey" on me in the bogs, and if you've got any samples of said smarties going spare por moi?'

Will reached into his pocket and then shook Dave's hand, palming him two pills as he did this.

'Cheers, Dave, you're golden you are mate!'

'Thank you, for your generous donation sweetie-pie! I'm sure Guido and I shall have fun with these magic beans later!' Now, what can I get you two party animals to drink? I'm feeling fabulously generous now that the beautiful people have arrived!'

Dave held his hands up together as though he was about to pray and bowed slightly towards Mel and Will.

Will threw a smile at Dave.

'Cheers, mate, I'll have a vodka and coke. Mel?'

'The same please, Dave, and may I just say, you are a such a sweetheart and not in the least bit sinister!'

Dave signalled to Guido and smiled at Mel.

'Why thank you, precious, you are such a cutie-pie! The sinister tag is just a little joke for the locals about those of us who choose to follow in the ways of Sir Elton. They think us queens are all a bit sinister so it fits in snugly with their Daily Mail-reading philosophy of the big bad world, ah, Guido honey, fix these two outrageously handsome beings two large vo-co's baby, and another Martini for me, isn't he just to die for Mel? And he's all mine so hands off Will! Ha-ha-ha!'

Mel looked at Guido and surveyed his classic Latin looks, jet black hair, smooth olive skin and large brown eyes with long feminine lashes and perfect white teeth which he flashed at her in a seductive smile.

'Mmm...he's pretty damn dreamy alright!'

'Oy! I am still stood here you know!'

Will put on a pouty expression of pretend hurt.

'Aww! Don't be jealous, baby, I think you're even dreamier!'

Mel linked her arm into Will's and kissed him gently on the lips.

'Now, now, my babies! Save that lovey-dovey stuff for later or I might vom into my Martini which would really be a tragedy! Right my darlings! I'm off to mingle, my public needs me and I must satisfy their desires for some Dave-love! You understand, cherubs? You two have fun and I'll see you later!'

Dave kissed them both on the cheek and waved his drink at them as he about-faced, waved at a group of people sat next to the dance floor and headed towards them.

A funky re-mix version of Eniac's *Pumpin* boomed out across the club. Will took a large gulp of the dark brown liquid in his glass and smiled at Mel.

'Let's dance, honey.'

Three hours later they moved in unison towards the double bed in Mel's room at The Highcliff.

Their tongues intertwining and hands moving over clothes, they undressed each other slowly and deliberately before collapsing together semi-naked onto the bed. He kissed her gently at first and then deeper. His lips moved to her neck and he felt her body shiver, he could feel his body melting and tingling with hot and cold sensation. Their kisses building like the swell waves of an approaching storm at sea. He moved over her body and she arched her back to meet him like a reed bending in the wind. He tracked slowly down her torso with soft kisses, his senses revelling in the delicate and sweet perfume of her skin. He brought his head between her thighs and Mel trembled and sighed as his mouth moved closer to her moist opening and she felt every nerve ending in her body was tingling with warmth and energy and as he sucked and licked at her clitoris. She felt as though she was floating on a cloud, flying like Icarus, closer and closer to the sun but not caring as its rays melted her wings. It was as though she were outside of reality and removed completely from her body but at the same time, more connected and in touch with every sensation and emotion of her physical being than she had ever been before.

Mel moved her hand to her mouth and bit gently on the knuckle of her forefinger as she felt her legs begin to shake and then her whole body begin to tremble as her orgasm began and she came with waves of colour flashing behind her closed eyelids. She quickly grabbed at Will's head and pulled him upwards. He responded and moved back up her body until his mouth met hers again.

Mel reached down and guided his cock into her, and it was Will's turn to moan with pleasure as he felt the heat and wetness of her cunt grip and draw in his engorged prick.

He felt every movement of her body charge him with electrical energy, like small lightning strikes were hitting him all over and zapping his body and he didn't know whether to move in her or stay still.

He was totally lost in her and he didn't want to be found, wanting to stay in her, joined with her forever but also knowing that the almost unbearable longing and desire to move was overwhelming him like a tidal wave.

Then they began to gently move together, both their bodies melting, like two scoops of ice-cream in a hot bowl, into each other.

They lost all sense of time and space as they moved, slowly at first, then faster and faster. Two independent raindrops, gathering side by side on a pane of glass then suddenly converging and accelerating earthwards to explode in a large dramatic splash at bottom of the window.

Will could feel Mel's body begin to shake, and he could feel his body responding as he neared orgasm. Their moans became louder, bodies moved more urgently together as they raced towards climax. Then he felt his whole body stiffen, lights danced across his vision and he cried out as he felt the hot liquid gushing deep inside Mel.

Mel's second orgasm came just after Will's and she felt as though she was floating and rising off the bed with Will still inside her, she cried out then bit down on his shoulder as her back arched, her arms and legs gripping his torso, as though she were a castaway clinging to a piece of wreckage, knowing that her life would be forfeit if she were to let go.

They both clung on together, still kissing and caressing as their bodies slowed down and recovered from the heat of their love making.

They stayed that way for a long time. Allowing the aftershocks of their orgasms to continue, not wanting the pleasure or closeness to end.

'Wow!' panted Will.

'Wow indeed!' panted Mel in response.

Thirty minutes later they did it again.

Then an hour later they did it again.

Then they were a bit knackered so they slept for four hours, woke up, and did it again.

Will propped his head on his elbow after he had recovered from their latest tussle, he ran his hand lightly on her naked flank, gently stroking and caressing with his fingers.

'You are really something special you know, babe, I don't

think I've met anyone quite like you before.'

Mel eyed him quizzically.

'Oh yeah? I bet you say that to all the girls!'

She poked him playfully in the chest. Will smiled and gave a guilty cough.

'Okay, okay, I *might* have said that before but I really do think you're different'

'You mean you were lying to all those other poor girls? Oohh! You absolute cad!'

'Stop teasing, Mel, I'm trying to be serious here, I'm trying to tell you I think there's something different about you. I felt a connection with you as soon as I saw you, like there was something we shared, some kind of secret. Sorry, I know that sounds really corny.'

'Yes you're right it does sound corny.'

Mel bit her lip and searched Will's face.

'Corny but sweet, now cuddle me and we'll get some sleep, we can talk more later.'

She stroked Will's face tenderly and kissed him gently before turning around so they could spoon. Will moved into her back kissed her ear and the back of her neck and wrapped an arm around her front which she hugged to her chest.

Does he know? How could he unless he's working with the contractor? It's too big a coincidence...besides he's lived down here for ages. But I'll have to tread carefully, I don't want to give away too much...and I like him, I like him a lot...oh shit! I'm in big trouble...Mel you silly cow! Why do I get myself into these messes? Shit, shit, fuckedy shit! I'll have to sort something out tomorrow.

Will looked at the soft curve of her neck and shoulder as she lay on pillow

She's hiding something, could she know about SUBDL? An under-cover cop? Doesn't seem likely, there is something though, Drugs Squad checking up on me? Nah, doubtful, she is different, and I like her, I like her a lot...shit Will! How do you get yourself into these situa-

tions? I'm going to have to be careful, I'll think of something tomorrow.

Kelly drove the Audi the two miles from the safe house to the lock-up garage. She took the rucksack and A4 envelope from the back seat and changed quickly next to the car. She put on the large hoopy gold ear-rings and fastened the thick nine-carat-gold solid curb chain around her neck. She quickly slipped into the blue Kappa tracksuit and stepped into her white, ladies Reebok Classics. She quickly applied some blue eye-shadow and checked herself out in the wing mirror.

There! From Assassin to business professional to Walthamstow council estate single mum in a few easy moves! Lookin' hot, Kelly babes!

She threw the rucksack back into the car along with the business suit, locked up the garage and headed round the corner to where her slightly battered, second-hand Ford Focus, complete with fluffy dice and stick-on window tints, was waiting for her.

The Audi was way too flash for a single mum who worked part time in an old people's home, she sagely knew that it would have brought unwelcome attention from her friendly but overly-nosey neighbours.

Kelly opened the envelope that she had picked up from the dead drop at the Swindon safe house and pulled out the printed list of instructions. She couldn't see a photo attached so she shook the envelope. A small black plastic credit card that had a bar code and "PROPERTY OF HIGHCLIFF HOTEL" stamped across the front fell out but no photograph materialised so she went back to the note from Barnaby and read.

Hello again, Angels, Charlie here...sorry Kelly, I've always wanted to do that but my American accent sounds more like a drunken Antipodean who's had all his teeth knocked out.

Anyway, back to the plot. You will probably have noticed by now the lack of a photograph for this job, well done, my clever little vixen! Go to the top of the class!

The reason for this is simple, you won't need one.

To explain, the hit is being contracted by the target! Strange world we live in eh? I think it's some kind of insurance thingy but I'm not entirely sure. All you need to know is that it's completely kosher as I know the intermediary contact personally and he's assured me that the target will be willing and waiting on the balcony of room 23, fourth floor of the Highcliff Hotel in Seafordby (lovely little seaside town, you should take time to explore!) at precisely seven-thirty on Sunday the 4th of October.

As the room overlooks the sea from the cliff top (hence the staggeringly unoriginal hotel epithet) I would suggest that a close shot with a high-velocity weapon should take care of the ballistic evidence but I'll leave the details in your very capable hands.

You'll have to acquire a maid's uniform from the staff room on the ground floor, (I've marked the staff changing rooms for you on the floor plan printed overleaf), but the little plastic door pass will give you "access all areas" status, and as the hotel bar and restaurant are open to non-residents it should not prove too difficult a task.

See, told you it was simple didn't I, my little flower?

The money has already been paid over so I'll forward it to your account on completion, plus there's the added bonus of the fact that if the target gets cold feet and backs out you still keep the fee. I'd call that a win-win situation, unless you'd rather not take on the job? Ring me on the usual number if you're not interested, but if I don't hear from you by the end of this week I'll take it as read that you are taking the job on.

Bon chance, mon ami!

Your ever faithful servant. B.

Kelly shrugged, *takes all sorts I s'pose...still, I won't need to do any more jobs this year and sixteen grand will have Christmas well covered.*

She placed the letter and card back in the envelope and walked to the car.

I'm sure Darren will be able to look after the girls that weekend, I'll just tell him I'm pulling a double sleep-in shift at Willow Trees that weekend to get the twins something nice for Crimbo.

Kelly unlocked the car, swung into the driver's seat and put the key into the ignition. Then she leant over to switch the radio to the news channel to see if there were any reports about dead High Court judges.

Chapter Three

The church and friary of St Francis stood at the northern end of Seafordby. It was wedged between the main road into the town, and the small, fast-flowing stream that ran along the base of the valley, before it dribbled its way across the centre of the beach to be swallowed hungrily by the sea.

Deep in the cellars below the old friary, Father Enrique Fernandez adjusted the video camera on the tripod and checked that the battery level was showing as full. He looked through at the viewing screen to make sure that the light was okay and the image of the man strapped to the solid wooden chair was clear.

He filled a glass of water from a large jug, ice tinkling as he poured and then placed the jug back on the table next to the camera. He crossed the floor of the large square room in the cellar and stopped a few feet to the left of the naked man slumped forward in the chair.

Then he quickly stepped forwards and grabbed the man's ear, yanking his head back quickly and throwing the glass of water in the man's face as he pulled it back.

'Wake up Patrick!'.

The man woke suddenly, spluttering and coughing from the icy water. And stared, puzzled at the sight of his parish priest stripped to waist.

'Wha the fugg! ... Where am I? ... Father Fernandez?!'

He looked down at the leather straps fastening his wrists to the arms of the chair and struggled against the bonds.

'What is this? ... Why am I naked? ... Let me go you evil fucker!'

Patrick had a fuzzy memory of the previous night. He'd visited Fernandez to explain how he was sorry he'd missed him after mass on Wednesday, when they had agreed to meet to settle their business arrangement.

Then the priest had offered him a big tumbler of twelve-year-old Glenlivet single malt. He couldn't remember finishing his drink though, now his head was pounding with the worst hangover headache he had ever experienced.

Fernandez gave a hollow laugh that he thought struck just the perfect level of malice and foreboding, he liked malice and foreboding...it was his kind of thing.

You see, Father Enrique Fernandez firmly believed that he was a direct descendant of Cardinal Phillipe Lopez-Fernandez, one of Spain's most infamous Grand Inquisitors.

In reality, Father Fernandez's great-great-great-great-great grandfather had been one Juan-Ignacio Fernandez. A fairly successful pig farmer in Andalucia at the time of the Great Inquisition who had made a very nice living supplying high-quality pork to senior local clergy, thus avoiding any accusing fingers pointing in his direction.

After all, what infidel or heretic would go near pork, let alone breed the non-kosher beasts? It therefore served as a perfect cover for his part-time devil-worshipping, virgin-deflowering and occasional cross-dressing and he lived the quiet, happy, if slightly kinky, medieval life of a wealthy farmer and land owner.

The devil worship and cross dressing bit was probably where Father Fernandez got his nasty streak and his love of cassocks from though, even if he was quite oblivious of his true heritage.

'Hah-hah-hah! Really, Patrick, are you trying to tell me that you cannot guess why I have brought you here?'

He really did think that he sounded the part of the Inquisitor, his rich Iberian accent adding just the right amount of, perhaps, malice and foreboding? Yes, that was it.

Patrick wondered why Father Fernandez was talking in that funny way and sounding like he was trying to do an impersonation of "the Count" from Sesame Street, so he shook his head in attempt to clear it, but it just made his headache worse. He stared hard at his parish priest, still not quite believing that this wasn't some kind of really, really vivid nightmare.

'Ummm, no not really, Father, well...there is that ten grand I borrowed from you, and I know I'm late paying you back and all that...but fuck sake, Father! Sorry...I mean for God's sake, Father! Isn't all this a little bit over the top? I'm doing me best to try and get the money together, honest I am, Father!'

Fernandez shook his head and sighed melodramatically.

'Patrick, Patrick, I thought I made eet clear that there would be consequences, malo...bad...consequences, if the money was not repaid on the agreed date? Times are hard for everybody, this global recession, eet ees hard for the church. We have had to look to other areas to survive, we must cambiar, change, yes? People no longer flock to our mother church and this ees muy, muy serious, you understand yes?

The multitudes turn away from the church and would prefer to believe in the material and scientific world, there ees no money in God any more, well, not in this country, the Third world and Latin America however, ees full of zopenco, you know thees word? It means estupida, stupid? Many of these people believe anything and understand nothing so eet ees simple to control them. They are weak and frightened and so, wherever you find weak, frightened and foolish people, there you will find the Catholic Church's focus and good business for us, but we are not in Latin America and my concern ees the churches financial business in this country and business for us here, ees not good. People here have heard of Charles Darwin and that bastado Meester Richard Dawkins, so eet ees more difficult to convince them that an old man with a big white beard created the world in six days, then went on vacation for a few thousand years.

So, here we struggle to make any money for our beloved fuhrer, I mean Holy Father, ha-ha, I always get this mixed up...excuse my small jokings, and yet you, Patrick, you still choose to enter into this arrangement with me. This ees the church's money, Patrick, the Holy Roman Church, the faith you were born into, and you defile and desecrate the church by stealing from it!'

As he finished speaking, Fernandez swung back and smashed the empty glass into Patrick's face.

Patrick screamed as he felt his nose shatter and the shards of glass tear into his face. Then he started to feel the agony of his injuries and he continued to scream even louder as the pain receptors in his brain went into overdrive.

'Scream away, Meester Gallagher, no one can hear you, I soundproof this cellar myself and eet has, unfortunately, been tested many, many times by defilers, heretics and sinners such as you. The Franciscan Brothers who built this church and friary were good solid builders, so the walls, they are very, very thick my friend...much like the Franciscans...all that "love of poverty" bull-sheet! We all know my Jesuit Brotherhood are the real power in the church, eh, Patrick?'

After a while Patrick became hoarse and tired from screaming and began crying and whimpering.

'Please, Father...let me go...how can you do this? ... Show me some mercy...this is a terrible sin, Father...you are a man of God.'

'God!'

Fernandez shouted angrily, he ran to the table and picked up a rubber tent-peg mallet, he turned and ran back to where Patrick was immobilised in the torture chair and was staring at the fat rubber hammer, wide-eyed with terror, as Fernandez swung down with the mallet on Patrick's exposed left foot, shattering the two smallest toe's into a jammy mess of blood, gristle and bone.

'What the fuck has God got to with this!"

Patrick screamed again before he passed out from the pain and shock of his injuries.

He wasn't to know it yet, but he would be woken several times after passing out from his torturer's attentions and allowed to plead for his life before being subjected to increasingly cruel and medieval punishments.

Five hours later, an out of breath and bloody Fernandez put the blow-torch and metal skewer that had finally finished his victim off on the cellar floor, untied the leather wrist straps and pushed Patrick's severely mutilated, bloody corpse forwards out of the chair and onto the large black plastic tarpaulin he had placed in front of his victim. He wasn't bothered about the ten grand as he had taken Patrick's wallet and car keys and forced him to sign over all his worldly goods to the Church and given Fernandez power of attorney (before Fernandez had got to the stage of removing his fingers) so the Organisation of Grey Fathers would most likely realise forty or fifty grand profit from their little "business arrangement". Patrick was always going missing for weeks at a time on drinking and gambling binges so his family would not think it unusual for him to be missing and it would probably be a month before they started to worry and contacted the authorities. Then Enrique would step in and offer the family the caring and secure bosom of the church. His superiors would be pleased.

He wiped the sweat from his forehead and walked to the video camera, pressed the "stop" symbol on the side and returned to the body, pausing to pick up the chainsaw and turn on the portable DVD player sitting on the table.

The sound of Shakira's "these hips don't lie" filled the cellar and Fernandez joined in and sang along cheerily, doing a few salsa moves as he started up the chainsaw and began cutting up Patrick's body.

The saw made easy work of the dismemberment and thirty minutes later a bloody and tired, but satisfied Father Enrique Fernandez hummed as he pushed a wheelbarrow full of body parts along the corridor of the presbytery cellars, towards the room that held the old coal-fired furnace.

I wonder what Mrs Phelan is cooking me for tea tonight? I hope eet ees not her attempt at paella again, how that silly Irish bitch can makes such of the pigs arsehole with a simple dish I never understand...no mind! I can get rid of her early and jerk off while I am watching how I muffled Patrick's screams by feeding him hee's dick! Hee, hee!

Patrick Gallagher had been right when he had called him an evil fucker.

Will woke up and looked across at the space where Mel should have been. He turned his head and sleepily looked around the room and saw her standing on the balcony. She was dressed in one of the hotel's white towelling robes and sipping intermittently from a coffee cup.

When she had woken up, Mel had looked across at Will and smiled at him sleeping. He looked so peaceful and childlike and she thought how strange it was, that blankness of expression, innocence and lack of care or concern that people's faces take on when they are in deep sleep. She rose carefully and quietly from the bed and crossed to the shower.

She stepped into the stream and let the wonderful warmth tingle through her as the water revived and stimulated her body. Then she remembered that she had less than two weeks to live and her tears began to flow as freely as the river of water coming from the shower head.

Her legs felt like jelly and she crumpled to the floor of the shower, and she felt small, as though she was shrinking to the size of an insect, terrified and helpless, trembling and crying as she lay on the tiles like a spider being washed down the plughole.

She recovered enough to finish showering after what seemed to her like an eternity and was now feeling numb, almost zombie-like as she went through the motions of making a coffee and then moving to the balcony to drink it. The jaw-droppingly stunning views of Seafordby Bay failed to lift her and only seemed to remind her of everything that she was soon to give up.

'Mornin' lover.'

Mel winced at Will's voice, then forced herself to smile before looking over her shoulder at Will.

'Finally decided to wake up then?'

'Sorry, honey,'

Will replied, as he stretched out in the bed.

'I was out for the count, have you been up long?'

'No, about half an hour, I've just boiled the kettle if you want to make yourself a coffee.'

Will cocked his head quizzically to one side like a puzzled puppy.

'Are you okay? It's just that you seem a little down this morning, you're not having regrets about last night are you?'

'God, no!' Mel reacted with a big grin.

'I'm just a little...preoccupied, hung over and coming down off the pills as well I suppose. Why, are you always cheery in the mornings?

Please don't tell me you're one of those people who don't get hangovers. I can't stand blokes bouncing around the morning after a heavy session like Graham Norton on speed, it's really fucking tiresome.'

Will laughed, then moved quickly from the bed and over to the dressing table to make a coffee.

'No worries there, babe, I feel like shite, my head's pounding and my mouth feels like I've been chewing brick-dust sarnies all night.'

Mel moved over to the bed, arranged the pillows so she could lean back against the headboard then plonked down on the bed, let her white robe slip around her shoulders to give extra support to her back and drew her knees up to her stomach.

'Good, I don't really do cheerful before mid-day. There are some paracetamol in my bag on the dresser there, bring the packet over with you, hun, I could do with some headache relief myself.'

Will fished in the bag and found the packet of tablets then headed back over to the bed with his coffee and handed them to Mel before climbing back under the duvet and planting a kiss on Mel's neck.

'It was a great night though wasn't it? I mean…we did have fun and everything?'

It was Mel's turn to look quizzical.

'Of course we did, why? What's with all the self-doubt stuff? Are you sure you're not trying to convince yourself you had a good time?'

'No, no…it's just I wondered if you felt the same way as I did you know? And I was doing some thinking.'

'Uh-o! Dangerous game that thinking business!'

Mel playfully patted Will on the top of the head.

'Your poor ickkle brainy-wain will overheat and cause a melt-down.'

'Ha-ha, very humorous, no, I was thinking, I've got about a month's leave saved up and as things are slowing down now that the summer season is just about finished, I could take a couple of weeks, I'm sure Simon, my boss would be cool about it now that the bar is quieter and maybe we could, you know, sort of hang out together…for a bit'.

Will toyed nervously with the duvet and looked into his coffee cup. 'Unless of course you've got plans and stuff..or you'd rather not…it's just I thought…you know…we got on so well and that…and I like you a lot and I…you know…really enjoyed it last night and I'd kind of… like…you know…like to get to, know you a bit better and that.'

Will looked hopefully at Mel whose eyes had got wider and wider as Will had bumbled his way through his plan. It took all of her reserves not to start crying again as she reached over and stroked Will's face.

'I'd really, really like that Will…I'm just not sure…I really like you too.

So how about I say yes now, but I may change my mind, I don't really know if I want to be on my own or with someone at the moment.' *Mel, what are you thinking? Do I really want to get close to him before I have to give it all up, is this fair on him?*

Oh shit, just go with flow, I don't have enough time left for things to get too complicated, plus I fancy him something rotten.

'There is one thing I'll have to insist on though.'

Will looked expectantly at Mel.

'What's that?'

'You have to stop bloody saying "you know" all the time, oh...and I want your body on demand as well, so you better be up for lots and lots of sex!'

Mel put her coffee cup down on the bedside cabinet, leaned over and took Will's cup, placing it next to hers before rolling back over onto Will and kissing him hard on the mouth, quickly throwing off her bathrobe as she moved to straddle him.

Chapter Four

'Right then, tell me a bit about yourself then. I mean, if we're going to be spending the next couple of weeks together I want to know that you're not just a really shallow and boring barman who hits on random women who happen to cross his path? Oh, and make it exciting or else you are sooo dumped!'

It was three in the afternoon and the couple were sat in "Toms' Diner" at the bottom of the hill from the Hotel tucking into a "Toms Special All Day Breakfast".

Will finished munching on the piece of greasy sausage, swallowed, and smiled at Mel.

'No pressure then? Okay, well I was born in the Nam.'

Mel looked surprised.

'You were born in Vietnam?'

'Naw, Chippen-Nam.'

Mel laughed.

'Good one, please continue.''Well, then I moved down here when I was sixteen to go the local college and basically to get away from my parents.'

'You didn't get on with them, then?' Mel interrupted.

'It wasn't that really, I just couldn't stand all the arguments and constant sniping back and forth. I don't even know how they manage to stay married. I don't know why people do that, stay together when they can't stand each other. It never made any sense to me. I guess it's fear of having to start again, find someone else or just fear of being alone, they're still living together and arguing their lives away in deepest Wiltshire.'

'Hmm, maybe they secretly enjoy the sniping and arguments?'

Mel picked up a sausage and waved it around absently as she spoke, taking the occasional bite.

'Yeah, you could be right there. Anyway, I passed my A-levels, barely, and went to London, UCL to do a degree in European history, but I ended up in jail instead.'

Mel dropped her sausage and her jaw at the same time.

'You what? ... What happened?'

'Well, basically I got into trouble in my final year in that I was completely skint and about twenty-six grand in debt, so I started selling eccy to mates at uni and down here. It seemed like a good idea until I got caught with about a hundred pills outside a mate's house and got three years for possession of a class-A substance with intent to supply.'

'Shit! You're a dealer then?'

Mel looked at Will intently.

'Naw, not really, and certainly not any more, once bitten and all that, I never carry more than four pills at any time now and I use those straight away, as you know from last night. The police were really after the guy supplying them to me, but he got tipped off by the police contact he was selling to and skipped the country before they could collar him. Luckily no one down here knows anything about it so I was able to get work in bars through college friends, then I got the job working for Simon at the hotel 'cause I was at college with his daughter, and she said I was cool because I looked after her when she got a bit too pissed at a party once. That's about it really, oh, I finished the degree in prison and did a Tefel course as well...oh – and I'm pretty good at darts.'

Mel sniggered.

'Darts, wow...will you be representing us at the London Olympics then? Bloody hell that's a life skill that's bound to come in handy!'

'Oh...you'd be surprised how handy, but no, sadly I won't be one of Lord Coe's hopefuls...I'm not altogether sure that darts is actually recognised as an Olympic sport yet, probably only a matter of time though. I've never played above county level 'cause me wrists were never strong enough...I knew I should have spent more time tossing off when I was a teenager!'

Will winked at Mel and took another mouthful food.

'What's a Tefel then, isn't that what they use to coat saucepans?' asked Mel.

Will shook his head and took a quick slurp of tea.

'Erm...no, that's Teflon, TEFL stands for Teaching English as a Foreign Language. I thought it would come in handy if I ever did a bit of travelling.'

'Oh...I see...well I kinda remember reading about Tefels on the internet.'

Will looked up from his breakfast.

'Oh you're not a secret computer geek are you?'

Mel smiled.

'Nah, I'm not one of the Twitterati, I think anybody who spends their free time sat in front of a blinking screen on a site that begins with the word 'Twit' rather than out meeting real human beings deserves their ivory tower, but congratulations! I'm still awake and it was a reasonably interesting life story I suppose, if a little brief...and dodgy criminal activity I'm not sure about either. Any other skeletons in the closet? Bodies buried in motorway bridges? Dodgy sexual liaisons with senior politicians on Hampstead Heath, you know, helping them to fill out their expenses claims for "entertaining"?'

Mel made little quotes signals with her index and middle fingers.

Will laughed and shook his head.

'No, sorry to disappoint, but I've never shared a room with William Hague, or Peter Mandelson, or Tony Blair...shit....he'd drive you mad with all those exaggerated arm movements and fake smile and saying "in all honesty" and "let me be honest when I say..." , what's that all about anyway? It kind of gives the game away that he was being dishonest all the times before then doesn't it?'

Mel laughed.

'Yeah. I just wish the phoney fucker would just go away and crawl up George Bush's arsehole, he spent so much time kissing it when he was prime minister he'll be in familiar territory at least, and maybe he might give Bush cancer of the colon with all that bile he comes out with. Mind you, Cameron and Obama aren't much better... Right, I'm bored of politics now, where are we going to go to tonight then lover? I fancy the funfair, I can cream you at dodgems and we can go on the waltzer after eating loads of junk and see who pukes first, hee-hee!!'

'Charming...I am still eating here, honey.'

Will pointed at his half eaten breakfast with his fork.

'Okay, funfair it is then, betcha you vom first though, I'm a Waltzer veteran, but seeing as I've just given up my dark secret past its now your turn to spill the beans on yours...so? Let's hear it then, former topless modelling career? ... Kicked out of Girl Guides for lesbian affair with Brown Owl? There must be something with shock value in your past, eh?'

Mel paled slightly and looked nervous for a split second but managed to recover before Will looked up from his breakfast with a grin.

'Oh there's nothing that exciting from me, sorry to your burst your pervy girl-on-girl fantasy bubble but I grew up on a council estate in Slough, the world's most boring town, friendly bombs and all that Betjeman stuff. School was fairly normal and I did okay, but nothing spectacular as exam results go. Not been to uni though, hmm let's see... I've got one older sister, both parents still alive and now happily retired to Bournemouth. Dad was a taxi driver and mum was a full-time housewife and mother. I went to live in Ibiza for a couple of years when I was eighteen, worked in a bar and as one of those annoying gits handing out drinks coupons to try and attract guys into the clubs. Then I moved back to London and started temping in offices and eventually I got a permanent job as a clerk for an insurance broker where I've been for the last five years. Bit dull really, but

I do tend to party hard to make up for the dullness.'

Mel shrugged and picked up her mug of tea.

'Sorry to disappoint but there's really no major scandals.'

'Aha, party girl, well, bet you've got some good Ibiza stories?'

Mel smiled mischievously.

'I might have, but I'll save those up until I know you a bit better don't want to give you all the juicy bits too easily, babe, you'll have to remain in suspense for the time being. Now finish you're breakfast like a good boy, you'll need all your energy to keep up with me.'

Mel winked seductively at Will and cradled her mug in both hands.

Will gave a little salute by raising his knife to his forehead and then ploughed back into his breakfast.

'Yes ma'am!'

Kelly smiled as she watched Destiny and Harmony's faces react to the cartoon characters on the massive wide screen plasma television. The two four-year-olds were completely mesmerised as Atomic Betty beat the living crap out of Alien Invaders for the hundredth time, *if only all of life's problems could be sorted out by Atomic Betty, what a great world that would be, I'd be out of the assassin business though...bummer.*

Kelly turned her attention back to her laptop and she re-checked her bank balance. The remainder of the fee for the hit on Judge Edwards had now been credited to her account and things were looking decidedly healthy on the financial front. Kelly figured that another two years and she could buy a nice house in Chingford or Epping, move the girls to a private school and retire from the assassin business and maybe go back to college, then maybe even university?

It wouldn't be too far away for Darren to come and visit but it would be close enough to the countryside to make her feel more comfortable.

She picked up her mobile and hit the contact number for Darren.

'Darren's phone.'

'Oh, it's you....could you put Darren on please?' Kelly snapped tersely.

She didn't like Brittany, Darren's new girlfriend and hadn't liked her from their first meeting which had gone something like this:

Darren: Right, Kelly? This is Brittany...she's um...my new girlfriend.

Kelly: Oh...right, alright?

Brittany: Awl right.

Kelly: Where you from then?

Brittany: Round 'ere innit.

Kelly: Don't I knows you from somewhere?

Brittany: Nah, don't fink so.

Kelly: Yeah, your Stacey Galvin's daughter ain't ya? From Hoxton Park?

Brittany: Yeah, so what if I am?

Kelly: Nuffin, just saying I knows you is all. No need to get all feisty.

Brittany: I ain't! Who you calling faisty? Bee-atch!

At this point, in one smooth quick movement, Kelly grabbed the finger with the elaborately decorated false nail that Brittany was pointing towards her chest, bent it swiftly upwards, twisting the wrist at the same time and then spun Brittany's arm downwards and around ninety degrees forcing Brittany's body to spin around after it until she was backed tight up against Kelly's chest and she could feel the tiny blonde pushing her arm further and further up her back.

'Ow!ow! That hurts you bitch! Darren! Don't just stand there, do sumfink you tosser!'

Darren looked sheepishly down at his shoes, he knew that all his girlfriends got "The Speech" as he called it, and despite his warnings to them to be civil and pleasant when meeting Kelly for the first time, they all made the same mistake of thinking this scrawny little blonde was no match for them.

Kelly pushed Brittany's arm up higher, making her squeal in pain and then leant in closely to her ear.

'Listen up you ugly ho...see my little gels over there? I'd do anyfing for them, absolutely anyfing to keep them happy and safe, see? I knows you and your family so if you ever so much as raise your voice to my gels, I'll fuckin' destroy you...ask your uncle Terry about me, yeah that's right darling, I know bad boy Terry Galvin, just tell him Kelly Black sends her love and watch his face!"

Kelly released Brittany and gave her a hard shove which caused her to lurch forwards into Darren's arms. A now tearful Brittany beat a fist against Darren's chest and threw a defiant look over her shoulder at Kelly.

'Good,' said Kelly. 'Now that we're straight on that, I'll pick the gels up on Sunday evening okay, Darren?'

'Okay, Kells'...see ya Sunday.'

Kelly really didn't like the girl one bit, but she knew that as soon as Brittany spoke to her uncle Terry, he would blanch and reach up to his shoulder as the memory of how she had driven a stiletto heel right through it and pinned him to a door. He had tried it on with her outside the back of a Walthamstow pub one night when she was fourteen and on the run from her third foster family in six months.

Kelly smiled to herself as she noticed a slight tremble in Brittany's voice as she responded to her call.

'Oh...hi Kelly, I'll just go get him for you...' there was a brief pause as Kelly heard a muffled angry exchange before Darren took the phone from Brittany.

'Hi, Kelly, the gels okay?'

'Yeah fine, Darren, I'll put them on in a mo to say hi, look I need a favour, babe. I've pulled an extra weekend shift at Willow

Trees on the third and fourth of October, I know it's my turn to have them that weekend but I wanted to get 'em sumfing special for Christmas this year, and I'll have them for an extra weekend whenever you like?'

'Hang on, Kells, I'll check.'

Kelly heard another muffled angry exchange for a few minutes and Darren came back on the phone.

'Yeah, okay then but you owe me for this, Kelly, and Brittany won't let me forget it either.'

'Cheers, Darren, I'll make it up to you, babes, honest... I'll just get the gels for you... Harmony! Destiny! ... Your dad's on the phone!

The two girls jumped up and ran to be the first to grab the phone with unified choruses of, 'Daddy! Daddy!'

Kelly held the phone out of the reaching little arms.

'Harmony's turn to go first, babe, you can go first later when he calls at bedtime, Destiny!'

Destiny scowled as Harmony stuck out her tongue and took the phone from Kelly.

Kelly turned and moved through the hallway into the kitchen. She crossed to the work surface and fished her other phone from her large brown Gucci bag.

She tapped out a text with one hand as she moved around the kitchen, opening cupboards, drawers and the fridge. The phone beeped to confirm that the message had been sent.

Barnaby reached into the inside breast pocket of his jacket when he felt it buzzing. He caught his breath as he puffed up the stairs towards his South Bank penthouse and paused to read Kelly's message.

Hi B! Will be tkin that break 2 cside we tlkd about. K.xx

Barnaby smiled softly.

'Good show, Kelly...jolly good show'.

Chapter Five

Will was in the mini-market just a few doors down from the Highcliff getting some munchies to take back to the hotel room. They had been smoking skunk on the balcony of Mel's room for the last hour and watching the sun go down when Mel had requested Pringles, Maltesers, sausage rolls and Iron-bru.

Will found himself craving some Curly Wurlies and cheesy Wotsits so had happily made his slightly stoned and wobbly way down to Asif's Mini-Market.

The last eight days with Mel had been magical and they had explored the town and surrounding area in his rusting old Peugeot, the engine straining as it climbed up and down the coastal roads and carried them to secluded coves and towns with funny sounding names that made Mel laugh. Will suddenly recalled one lunchtime as they were sat on a windy cliff top eating cheese-and-onion rolls and drinking cheap screw-top red wine, watching the sun play catch with cotton-wool clouds that scudded quickly away, as though scorched every time the hot globe touched them. Mel had been leaning back into his chest as he cradled her in his arms, both of them gazing out at the white horses racing each other in towards the bay.

'I wish I could just stay here forever, you know? Freeze time or something, this is so peaceful and quiet...so different from London, it's like a really special dream.'

Will hugged her closer.

'I know what you mean, even though I've been around the country a lot I've always felt drawn back to the sea, drawn back to this part of the world.'

'Yeah, but I kind of meant the moment as well, you know what I mean? Being here with you and the place, the view. I've always felt alone before, even when I was with someone, kind of like sneezing and no one being around to say "bless you"...you know what I mean?'I don't feel like that with you, I feel safe and warm inside, you're like a...like a...silky.'

Will looked at her puzzled.

'A what?'

'My security blanket that I had when I was little, I called it Silky, I went everywhere with it and used to cry and sit in front of the washing machine when my mum had to clean it 'cause it was bogging...that's my new nickname for you, Silky'.

Mel turned her head and kissed Will's cheek.

'That's sweet...weird, but sweet.'

Will kissed the top of her head.

Mel sighed.

'Yeah, well, that's me all over, weird but sweet. I'm really, really happy right now, though. Why do you think people are unhappy, Will?'

Will shrugged and held Mel a little closer.

'I dunno that they are unhappy, babe, most people are just a bit bored with their lives, they want something exciting to happen but are scared by what they see on TV or read in the papers. They think that the streets are full of drug dealers, or rioters and criminals who are going to murder, rape or steal from them. A vast underclass of the great unwashed, who are about to invade suburbia and redistribute all their precious possessions and wealth through violent and bloody revolution. The establishment like this thinking 'cause it helps to control the masses with fear, it's in their interest to keep people shut up in their homes and isolated, like being tagged...you know what I mean?'

Mel threw Will a half-smile.

'Hmmm...sounds like a cynical conspiracy theory to me, who do you mean by "the establishment" then?'

'Well I don't mean the government because that changes all the time, but senior civil servants are always in Westminster, aren't they?

And those fuckers in charge of the banks, you know, top

businessmen, captains of industry, anyone who has real money and influence.'

Mel looked back out at the blue Atlantic swells, they seemed to have a hypnotic and calming effect on her mood, she nodded.

'Maybe you're right, but I think there is something deeper there as well, people have this nagging ache at the core of their being that something is wrong with their lives you know? That something is missing, or we've lost our way somehow. That there has to be a bit more to life than work or family and all that everyday bullshit that we fill our lives up with.'

'Jeez, Mel...that's a bit fuckin' deep for me, I just try not to think about that, keep my shit together, hold on to the merry-go-round and have some fun along the way. I think we better head back to the hotel before you talk me into leaping over this cliff, which would kinda ruin my gorgeous looks and spoil what's been a perfectly blissed-out day, honey!'

Mel laughed and kissed Will's shoulder.

'Yeah, hun, you're right, ignore me I'm just being deep and meaningless, lets head back, I've had enough of the stunning vista's for one day.'

The nights at the Highcliff had become increasingly passionate, tender and comforting. But Mel sometimes had this sadness that Will couldn't altogether understand. He realised that he was already falling deeply in love with her and that he would have to tell her this before the end of her stay. It was too late for him now, and if she didn't feel the same way about him he knew that he was going to hurt inside and hurt badly.

He had been through holiday flings before but had never felt as strongly as this about anyone before. He had also had girlfriends in the past for varying lengths of time, the longest being for two years but this was very, very different. Mel seemed to possess this intensity and energy that he had never experienced before and the Plan B tune *Love goes down* came to mind when he thought about her. As he wandered through the aisles of the mini-mart humming the tune to himself he came to a decision.

I've got to tell her how I feel, it might fuck things up between us but I've got to let her know, about everything, about SUBDL, about being in love with her... If she doesn't feel the same then I'm gonna get hurt but fuck it! If she leaves without knowing I feel this way then..I don't know...this is mad! I've never been so scared of losing someone as this before, never cared about anyone like this... I just don't know how to go about telling her. Jesus, Will, you are sooo in over your head mate!

Will's phone buzzed like an angry wasp in his pocket, breaking his thought pattern and making him jump. He reached in and brought the phone to his ear.

'Hello?'

'Allo, West-Coast, you wankah! It's your old mate Billy ere, how's the surf-n'-turf business? Shagged any attractive lookin' sheep recently? Haw-haw!'

'Very funny, Soho, what do you want? Let me guess, you've run out of anal lube again and you want me to bring you up a hundred weight of surf-board wax?'

'Smart arse, just get your spotty carrot-crunching behind here next Friday at three pm sharp. You've got Anton "Pretty Boy" Golding in the Regional Final, okay, ranked number one at moment isn't he mate? Gotta dash kid, punters to rip off, women to debase, ciao, baby!'

The phone clicked dead and Will put it absently back into his pocket.

Anton, shit! He's not half bad. Still, I beat him last year, I'm sure I can turn him over again.

Will's victory over Anton had been in the first round of last year's championship and then he had got knocked out himself two rounds later.

Anton was a six-foot Jamaican man-mountain. He had been in Pentonville for money laundering when Will was inside and was reputedly a highly ranked member of a yardie gang in Balham, despite being a couple of years younger than Will.

He had been told to steer clear of him inside but when their paths had crossed, Will found him to be clever, polite and surprisingly softly spoken. Will liked him and they had become friendly through SUBDL Often practising together on the crappy prison dartboards. That meant it was always a tight game when they played in competition, but they both enjoyed the challenge and were always happy to play each other.

Mel crushed out the spliff in the ashtray and gazed out across bay as the pale yellow globe of sun disappeared over the headland to the west. She felt a sudden chill in the wind and used the balcony railing to haul herself up. A tear rolled down her face as she looked down to the empty sun terrace forty feet below the balcony, and she watched as the wind did its best to playfully pull the sun umbrellas over the railings at the far end of the terrace and then lure them the short distance to the waiting cliff edge.

She knew how they felt, pulled between life and death. She knew she could still back out, knew that she had complicated things with Will, but also knew that pulling out would mean the end for Kathy, that was the one thing she could not and would not accept.

She had thought that she would be able to keep herself together for two weeks, but every time she was alone and Will wasn't around, she seemed to be at an emotional breaking point as the sand in the hour glass trickled away towards her death, she had a sudden image of Dorothy in the witches castle from the Wizard of Oz when the scary green witch had turned the hour glass upside down.

It was a film that had always frightened her as a child, but the image paled now compared to the fear she was feeling.

Mel knew that this was how prisoners waiting on "Death

Row" must feel as their execution approached, had hoped that she would reach some kind of acceptance of her situation, and with that acceptance would come some kind of emotional stability or numbness. Her case was very different though in that all she had to do was walk out the door of the hotel at any point before Sunday the fourth of October and this would be all over for her.

But it would also mean the end for Kathy.

Mel crossed the room and slumped onto the bed, curling herself up in a ball.

Hurry up Will...I need you to be here, to hold me!

It was going to be harder than she had thought to let Will go now. The passion of their lovemaking had increased over the past week, maybe it was because she had so little time left that she was pouring every bit of herself into Will, and had never loved anyone so deeply or so desperately.

He stopped the clock ticking for her when he was with her, but as soon as she was alone, the realisation of her death would hit her and crush her like a nuclear wind.

I cant go on like this, I've got to tell him or get rid of him...it's fucking mad! I'm going fucking mad, shit, I don't know what to do...what if it fucks everything up between us? What am I going to do? I need him so much... I don't think I can make it through this week without him... I don't know how to tell him though.

The tears came harder now, and Mel curled up even tighter to try and stop the shaking that accompanied her sobbing.

Then the door opened and Will saw her.

He dropped the carrier bags and ran to the bed, cradling her in his arms.

'Shit Mel!...what the fuck happened? ... Who did this to you? What did this to you...shit! I was only gone twenty minutes...shhhh! Please baby, please don't cry... I'm here now, I love you...don't cry!'

Mel's shaking stopped and she turned to look at Will's face.

She knew then, she could see it in his eyes, beyond the shocked expression on his face.

'Wha..what did you just say?'

Will stroked the side of her face gently with the palm of his hand.

'I said don't cry,

then I said I love you.'

Mel managed to squeak out 'Oh shit...' before she buried her face in Will's chest and started crying again.

After about fifteen minutes Mel had calmed down enough to wash her face and was now lying across Will's legs and eating Pringles as he was propped up against the headboard by pillows and tucking into a Curly Wurly.

'Look Mel, there's something I've got to tell you'

'I know, I know, *you lurve me...you wanna do me!*'

Mel put on an American accent as she sang this to him, throwing Pringles at him at the same time.

'Fucksake Mel! I'm trying to be serious here, give me a break, honey.'

'Sorry, okay, go ahead, I'll be good, promise'

Mel crossed her heart with a Pringle, before stuffing it whole into her mouth.

'I'm just trying to say, you know, how I feel about you, and basically I don't want this fortnight to end. I've never felt like this about anyone before, I mean...I've been in love before, had girlfriends and that before, but it was different...you're different...do you get what I'm saying?'

Mel stared down at the hotel floor and nodded.

'It's just...I have to tell you something about me, something secret about me...and I'm not sure if I'm doing the right thing or not but I don't really care if it's right or not, but I just want to tell you because I want you to know everything about me.'

Mel turned her face to Will and saw that he was serious, and she saw fear in that expression as well. She was suddenly worried and frightened herself.

'Se-secret, Will? What do you mean secret?'

She could see that Will was nervous and that made her nervous, *is he the contractor?*

Will coughed slightly and lowered his voice.

'Well, you know I told you I was good at darts?'

'Yee-ees?'

Mel was now just puzzled.

'Well, when I was in prison I joined a secret underground darts

league called SUBDL or subtle, as we call it...'

Mel burst out laughing. When she saw that Will was being very serious she tried to control it to a giggle.

'Sorry Will...darts? (giggle), you mean like blokes in pubs with beer bellies throwing tiny bits of metal into circles of cork? (giggle), that kind of thing? (more giggling).'

'No...I mean yes! ... I mean it's not like that!'

Will was in a bit of a huff now, so Mel tried to stop giggling.

'Look, Mel, this is really serious, these guys, they would kill me for just telling you this, one guy I knew got two fingers and both thumbs cut off for trying to rig a game, another got his hand pushed into a milling machine in the prison workshop for threatening to go to the screws after he lost a load of money. These guys are deadly serious, there's a lot of money at stake but I just want out of the whole fucking thing!

I just want you...and I just want to be with you!'

Mel had stopped laughing when Will had started to talk about the hand injuries.

She moved from lying on Will's legs to a sitting position on the bed, drew her legs up to her chest, wrapped her arms around them and rested her chin on her knees.

'Oh Will...this is so difficult for me...I...I won't be around after this fortnight, baby, I have to go...go somewhere, I'm so sorry...I.'

'No! I'm not going to lose this now that I'm finally happy! I need to be with you!'

Will leant forward and wrapped his arms around Mel, hugging her tightly.

'You've been straight with me, Will, and you've confided in me so I'm going to be straight with you.'

Mel turned her face to look at Will who had a pained and desperate expression on his face.

'I need you too Will...when you're not near me I'm falling apart and there's a very good reason for this, but before I tell you about me...about what's going to happen to me, I want you to promise me...swear to me, that you won't try to interfere with what's happening, that you won't interfere with my plans'.

It was Will's turn to look puzzled and frightened.

'What are you on about, Mel? What's going to happen to you?'

'Swear, Will...swear to me you won't interfere.'

Will could see that Mel was serious and was struggling to hold herself together.

'Okay, okay...I swear I won't interfere with your plans...but I don't think it's fair for you to ask me to do that when you know I'd do anything to help you, you know that babe, don't you?'

Mel smiled slightly at this.

'I know, honey, that's why I made you swear. Well, here goes.'

Mel cleared her throat.

'I was eight years old and my sister was ten...we used to take this shortcut home from school if it was raining. We only lived fifteen minutes' walk away going the long way round, but taking the short cut halved the journey. Our mum had told us off one time when we had got caught using it, but we'd used it loads of times without them knowing it. My sister wanted to walk the long way round but I pestered her, I didn't want to get wet and would have whinged all the way home so she gave in. Part of the short cut meant we had to walk along the top of a railway embankment that bordered the main line into London for about a hundred meters. Loads of kids from our school used it, even though we'd been specifically told not to, we were just kids though, and it was a bit of a dare for us to do it. Well, we got about halfway along when I slipped and slid all the way down the embankment and...I, I...hit a bump or a ridge about ten feet from the bottom and got thrown up in the air and onto the railway line, breaking my arm in the fall.'

'Bloody hell, you must have been shitting it!'

Mel gave a little sad smile again.

'No...that's the really weird thing, my sister said I didn't make a noise during the whole fall, and I was only whimpering slightly when she got to me. You see, she slid down after me as soon as she saw what had happened and dragged me off of the railway line. About two minutes later a high speed train went right over the spot where I had been lying on the track.'

'Fucking hell!'

Will whispered slowly.

'Yeah...fucking hell is right. The train driver had spotted us and the police turned up five minutes later. Anyway, our mum went mental when she turned up at the hospital. I had my arm set and they gave my sister a tetanus jab because she'd cut herself scrambling over the fence next to railway line. We had to suffer the humiliation of having our mum walk us to and from school for the next six months. My sister was well mad with me. What with her having to be escorted to school like a baby and shown up in front of her friends. She got over it though and forgave me. What we didn't know at the time was that I'd managed to give my sister a death sentence.'

Will looked even more confused as the tears ran down Mel's face.

"I don't understand, what do you mean "death sentence"?'

'Something got into her blood stream from the cut on the fence, the doctors said that an animal must have cut itself on the fence not long before my sister cut herself and an infection transferred to her...and, and...the infection has mutated in her blood-stream, the doctors reckon she's got about twelve months, but there is a possible treatment.'

Will reached out and touched Mel's face tenderly.

'But that's good, isn't it? That means that there's still hope?'

Mel smiled at Will through the tears.

'That's why I'm here, the treatment is in a clinic in Austria, the only problem is that it costs one hundred and fifty thousand pounds, we've tried everything but we just can't raise the rest of the money, but...but I've solved that. My sister and brother-in-law have managed to raise ninety thousand from my parents, bank loans and fund raising, begging from every possible source, and I have a life insurance policy worth eighty thousand, so I can save her, I can finally repay her for saving my life.'

Will was now completely confused.

'But you can't get the life insurance money unless you're...'

'Dead?'

Mel nodded and wiped her face.

'I've told you this much, so you might as well know the whole story. I worked for a guy in Ibiza, he owned a bar and had "connections" with some very serious ex-pat people. He owed me a favour so he got in touch with this lawyer friend of his in London. I had twenty grand saved up, it wasn't enough to help my sister but it was enough to arrange my death.'

Will jumped up from the bed

'You fucking what? ... What the fuck do you mean your death?'

Mel was crying even more now.

'I'm...I'm so sorry Will, I'm sorry for dragging you into this mess but it was the only the way. Next Sunday at seven-thirty, I'm going to be standing on the balcony of this room, looking out to sea and someone is going to walk through that door and shoo...shoot me!'

Will crouched down on his haunches and covered his face

with both hands.

'No! ...No way! ... This is not fucking happening, this is not fucking happening!

What does this killer look like then? I'll kill him before he lays a finger on you!'

'No, Will...please, you promised me you wouldn't interfere, besides I don't know what they look like, I didn't even send them a picture of myself, just sent them the money, told them the room number and the time and date. It's too late to stop it happening now and they'll kill you as well if you get in the way, it's the only way to save Kathy, the only way I can make it up to her.'

Mel started to shake.

'Please...please Will..I'm so sorry...just hold me Will please...I'm so sorry...'

Her sentence tailed off as her sobs overcame her.

Will crossed to the bed and hugged Mel tightly, tears now running down his face as well.

'Shhhh, please don't cry, baby...I'll stay with you...I...I can never leave you now.'

They held each other tightly until the crying and shaking stopped. Then they undressed and made love with an almost agonising tenderness, both of them crying at times and greedily savouring every caress, every sensation of each other's body before collapsing as though every emotion had been vampire-sucked out of them.

Hours later, Will turned to Mel and told her about the phone call from Soho Billy.

'So you'll have to go to London then?'

Mel looked worried.

'Yeah, but don't worry, hun, I'll get Sinister Dave to look after you for the day.'

'But I don't want you to go Will, I wish you could cancel it...but I don't want your hands mangled...so I guess you've got to go?'

'Sorry, honey, I'll try to be back as quick as possible.'
Will gave Mel a reassuring hug and kissed her shoulder.
A plan was already forming in his mind about what to do.
I need to speak to Dave, he'll help. I know he will...

Chapter Six

'I'm in a world of shit, Dave, I need to get hold of eighty grand in the next couple of days, I've got thirty grand saved but I'm going to need that for getting out of the country.'

Dave went pale and winced.

'That is most definitely a world of shit, sweet cheeks, eighty bloody grand! What have you got into? It's not tied up with drugs again is it?'

Dave and Will were sat at a table in the Blue Lagoon on a wet Monday afternoon, Mel was sat at the bar nursing a drink and repeatedly glanced over at the table a nervous smile on her face.

Will smiled back at her and waved.

'No, the money's not for me, Dave.'

He turned back to face Dave.

'It's for her.'

Dave's eye's widened like an owl that's just spotted lunch.

'Nooo! ... She looks so innocent, what's she done? She's not a murderer on the run for killing her husband is she?'

'No, mate, it's more complicated than that I'm afraid, just try not to look surprised and laugh every now and again while I'm explaining this, I've promised her not to tell anyone so don't stare at her.'

'Oh goody! I'm fantastic at games darling! Do carry on, I'm on tenterhooks!'

Sinister Dave managed to keep his cool and even laugh and touch Will's hand playfully as he listened with increasing shock to his friend's tale of Mel's predicament.

'Wow, poor Mel, what a horrible business, and poor you! You really are deep in the brown and smelly baby! And let me guess, you're in love with her?'

Will looked down at his hands and then desperately back at Dave.

'Totally...and I couldn't bear to lose her, Dave, it would be the end of me.'

Dave scratched his head.

'If I had the money, Willy dearest, I'd hand it over now, this has got to be the single most romantic and exciting thing that's ever happened in this crappy little burg and I'll do anything I can to help, but there's only one person I've heard of in this town who can access such an obscene amount of folding green at short notice, and I've heard some really nasty rumours about him. And when I say really nasty, I mean very very scary...like, imagine if you died and when you got down to the seventh circle of Hell you discovered that you had to spend all of eternity sat next to Jeremy Kyle, that scary!'

Will shuddered, 'Ughh! ... That is scary, Jeremy Clarkson would be worse though.'

Dave made a screwed up face.

'Yuk! Or Jeremy Paxman.'

Will nodded thoughtfully.

'Jeremy Beadle? He would be a bit irritating, and Jeremy Vine...or Jeremy Williams.'

Dave threw a puzzled look at Will.

'Who the hell is Jeremy Williams?'

'Kid in my class who used to bully me, total dickhead...here, do you think that there is some kind of factory throwing out evil Jeremy's controlled by some higher power and nobody's realised it?'

Dave chuckled.

'What do you mean by higher power? You're not suggesting Madonna's got anything do with this! Seriously though, baby, this guy is bad news, and he's not even called Jeremy.'

'Who is it?'

Dave searched Will's face and could see the determination in his eyes.

'Well, I've heard that a certain Father Fernandez at Saint

Francis church, you know the one up on Bristol Road? He can "help people out" if you know what I mean, but be really, really careful Will, he's dangerous, and there have been stories that he can make people disappear in very nasty and evil ways.'

Dave reached across and put a heavy hand on Wills arm.

'Thanks, Dave, I'll be careful, can you keep an eye on Mel for me while I go and see him? I'll be back as soon as I can, and I'll need you help me with something else if my plan is going to work.'

Dave was surprised.

'Plan? You've got a plan already? You are a dark and dangerous little rascal aren't you? Okay, it'll be a delight to take care of your gorgeous girl and of course I'll help you darling, I just hope your plan is an earth-shatteringly clever one!'

Two hours later, Will was sat in the back pew of Saint Francis church watching as a blue-haired woman, who must have been in her eighties he thought, made her way towards him down the centre aisle of the church with a large feather duster in her hand. She had a wonky eye, which was made more exaggerated by the badly applied shocking blue eye-shadow. As she got closer, Will could see the caked-on foundation flaking off her chin and a strong smell of Pledge polish, mixed with vodka and garlic filled his nose.

She smiled at Will, and some more chunks of foundation peeled away from the corners of her mouth.

'Hello, sonny...are ye after the Father?'

'Erm...yeah, thanks...is he about?'

'Yes, yes...I'll just go fetch him, you stay there, sonny, say your prayers.'

The strange smells of incense and the scary old lady had just succeeded in making Will even more nervous than he was before he had entered the church.

After what seemed like forever a tall and solidly built, dark-haired man in a black cassock who looked a bit to Will like an older version of Antonio Banderez, appeared from a door beside the altar and made his way down the centre aisle to where Will was seated. He stopped as Will stood up.

'Welcome to Saint Francis my son, how can I help you?'

'Father Fernandez?'

'Yes, that ees me.'

'I hear that you are a man who can help people who have financial, erm...problems?'

Fernandez smiled at Will, revealing a set of capped and perfectly white teeth.

'And who, may I ask, ees telling this to you?'

'Oh, I just heard, you know.'

'No matter, my son, please come with me, we can talk properly in my office where eet ees more...comfortable, yes? What ees your name, my son?'

'It's Will, Will Cummings, er,...yeah that would be cool, sorry, I mean good.'

Fernandez laughed.

'Please Will, I know what ees cool, I use this word also.'

He held out a palm to Will and they shook hands. Fernandez spun and walked off up the aisle, Will followed behind, still nervous at the strangeness of the church. He followed Fernandez past the altar, through the door he had seen the priest emerge from where they entered a long gloomy corridor, spanned by stone arches every ten feet. There were dark, thick oak doors intermittently to his left and arched windows along the right side of the corridor.

They stopped at one of these doors about halfway along the corridor. Fernandez turned the heavy black doorknob and swung the door inwards, holding the door for Will after he passed through it.

Will looked around the plush office. One wall was taken up from floor to ceiling with a solid bookcase, full of dusty and expensive-looking leather-bound volumes. There was a thick red pile carpet and a large oak desk sat in front of a huge stone chimney breast, with an open fire blazing and crackling in the hearth. Along the left wall of the room were two massive arched windows framed by Crimson red heavy drapes. Opposite the windows, silver metal filing cabinets book-ended a large rosewood sideboard with an ornate gilt mirror above it. Along the wall were large imposing oil paintings of sombre looking senior clerics in black robes. Will was surprised to find such an obvious display of opulence in a humble parish church, but he did his best to hide his astonishment.

Fernandez gestured to a comfortable leather armchair on one side of the desk.

'Please sit and be comfortable, my friend. Can I offer you a drink? I am having a Glen Morangie, do you like single malt wheesky, Will? Or perhaps a vodka and cola?'

'Erm... Vodka and cola please.'

Will sat down and watched as Fernandez opened a door on the sideboard to reveal an impressive variety of spirit bottles and crystal decanters, with differing levels of colourful liquids. He quickly prepared the drinks and handed a heavy tumbler to Will before rounding the desk and settling into his large executive leather chair.

He held his glass up.

'Salute! So, exactly how can I of service to you?'

'Erm...as I said before, I have a rather difficult financial problem that I need your help with.'

Fernandez toyed with the liquid in his glass and narrowed his gaze at Will.

'I believe I have seen you before around Seafordby, Will, perhaps at the Highcliff Hotel no?'

'Yes, that's where I work...but I don't remember seeing you in there?'

'I think I see you in a uniform, going in and coming out when

I am passing eet in my car. A few of my parish live near hotel, so I pass from time to time. This ees good that you work at this time, many people find eet hard to find work in a small town like this, but I know that we all have the money problems in good and bad times. So, how much money do you need?'

Will took a large slug of his drink and composed himself before looking up at Fernandez.

'It's a large problem for me, eighty thousand pounds large.'

Will watched for a reaction from Fernandez, the priest merely intensified his gaze towards his tumbler.

'Hmm, that ees a large problem, my friend, when do you need to have this money?'

'Well, as soon as possible, Father?'

Will was staggered by Fernandez's apparent nonchalance.

'I will need some personal details from you first of course, your address, bank details, your parents or other relatives details, and some other small information, I must carry out checks on you...you understand? It should not take too long, I can have the money for you in twenty-four hours, there will of course be a charge for the lending, it ees ten percent per day. I think this ees fair no?'

Will was doing his best to hold himself together.

'Err, yeah, that seems fine to me. I must admit, Father, I'm impressed that you can do all this so quickly.'

Fernandez smiled at Will and took a swig of his single malt.

'My friend, my brotherhood has been doing business in this ways for a long time. The Catholic Church must keep up with the times and we no longer rely on our flock to fund our many good works yes? We have had to "diversify" this ees the correct word I think? I am merely a humble servant of God and so must do what I can to make sure eet ees protected from financial problems yes?'

Fernandez stood and walked to one of the silver filing cabinets. Pulling open the top drawer, reached inside and took out a green folder and then walked back to the desk.

'Now, my friend, there are just a few papers I need you to complete and we can advance with our business.'

He opened the folder and removed a few pages of forms that were stapled together, and bore a line drawing of Saint Francis church as a logo in the top right of the front sheet. He offered the papers to Will and then offered him a very decorative fountain pen with a white six pointed star logo on the top end.

Will stared at the pen before looking at the papers.

'Erm, is this a Mont Blanc pen, Father?'

Fernandez sat in the chair and eyed Will with a slight smile of interest.

'You have a good eye Will, yes eet ees.'

'Shit...sorry, Father, I mean wow, it's just I've never seen one of these up close before, let alone held one...I bet it cost an arm and a leg?'

Fernandez smile grew wider and he seemed to Will to be enjoying some private joke with himself.

'Oh yes, my young friend, I can assure you eet cost more than a mere arm and leg.'

Will looked at the pen for a few moments longer then turned his attention to the forms. They seemed to be fairly basic finance forms, confirming his personal details and those of his next of kin and his bank details.

Will paused when he got to the section regarding his next of kin.

'Excuse me, Father, why is it you wanted my parents' details again?'

Fernandez, who had swung his chair towards the fire as Will had been completing the forms, now swung his chair back and eyed Will with a stern expression.

'My young friend, you are a stranger to me, you have come into my church and ask me for the loan of this large amount of money. It would be estupida for me not to check who you are and where you come from before I agree to this, and I am not the stupid man. I am sure that the person who told you about me also told you that there are certain "stories" about my business dealings in this town, yes?'

Will shrugged and his face flushed with embarrassment.

'Well, yes, now that you mention it...'

Fernandez leaned forward in chair and held a hand up to halt Will's sentence.

'Eet ees okay, Will, let me assure you that all of these stories are true. Please do not believe for one moment that were you to attempt to cheat me or steal this money from my organisation, that some terrible misfortune would not befall you and your family. Are you clear on this my friend, eet ees not too late to cancel our arrangement?'

Will could see that Fernandez was deadly serious and could feel the sweat trickling down his back inside his tee-shirt.

'Err, crystal clear, Father, I don't want to cancel, just err, you know, checking.'

Fernandez leant back in his chair and his wide smile returned.

'Excellent, my good friend, then we will talk no more of such things.'

Fernandez casually swung back to the fire, and Will tried to stop his hand from shaking as he returned to completing the paperwork.

He signed the document and cleared his throat as he placed the paperwork on the desk, carefully positioning the obscenely expensive pen on the top sheet.

Fernandez looked around at the documents and stood up to face Will.

'All ees een order now? Good, good! Once my checking ees done I will telephone you and meet you here tomorrow at nine pm. I am guessing you would like the monies in cash yes?'

Will shook his head.

'Erm...no, could you transfer it to this account number please.'

He pulled a crumpled piece of paper from his pocket and pushed it across the desk towards Fernandez.

Fernandez looked at the numbers and then compared them to the details on the completed forms.

'But this is not the same account as yours my friend?'

Will swallowed nervously.

'No, no it's a friend's account'

Fernandez looked puzzled and hesitant for an instant but then shrugged and smiled at Will. Maybe the money was not for drugs as he had first thought, or perhaps this young man was just being cautious in covering his tracks, had more about him than met the eye.

'No matter, the money ees yours to do with as you wish, as long as you have completed the section on the details of when you will be making repayment, yes?'

Will looked up at the priest, his face hardened into a grim expression.

'Yeah, don't worry, you'll get it all back.'

'Come, come, Will, do not be so downhearted, I am sure you will make this money work for you, and your problems will soon be over. I think you are a very resourceful man, yes? After all, you managed to find your way to me to help solve your business problems.'

Fernandez held a hand out and Will managed a weak smile as the big priest pumped his arm rapidly.

'Good, good! You will see, my friend, your problems are solved, we have a good business arrangement now. Please, do not worry about anything, I will take care of things by tomorrow night, you must trust me Will.

I have much work to do now on your behalf my friend so I think our business ees all finished for this evening yes? Please my friend, allow me to escort you out.'

As soon as Will was out of sight of the church he leaned on a low garden wall and vomited.

'Shit! ...Well that was way easily, the scariest fuckin' thing I've ever done in my life.'

By the time he got back to the Blue Lagoon Mel was totally pissed and doing a slow dance with Guido to Bowie's *Scary Monsters* which made Will laugh at the total randomness of the scene.

He went straight to Dave, who was behind the bar and smiling at Guido's slightly frightened expression, as Mel kept laughing while trying to feel his arse and cling to him. Guido meanwhile, was trying to hold her as far away from his body as he could.

Dave took one look at the pallid hue of Wills face and made him a very large Vodka and coke while he spoke.

'I won't ask how you got on, honey, as I can see from your face you need alcohol and stat!'

'Cheers, Dave, expert judgement as always mate.'

Dave prepared a second large drink as he watched Will down the first one rapidly, then Will's whole body gave a shudder as the burning sweet liquid disappeared from the glass.

'I'll make you another one in a minute, babes, but try to take this one a bit slower, eh? I'm not made of vodka, mores the pity! I could just pop myself in a glass and you could swallow me down in one gulp, you gorgeous boy!'

He stroked the back of Will's hand and winked suggestively.

Will managed a smile again.

'Dave, you really are stellar, you know that? You always know how to cheer me up. Guido's really lucky to have a guy like you looking after him.'

Dave's cheeks flushed and he fanned himself quickly with one hand.

'Oh shucks, sugar! Keep it to yourself, I've got my sinister reputation to uphold, but you are an angel for saying it, so I thank you most sincerely from the bottom of my chintzy under-garments. But speaking of my beloved, I think we better rescue him before your nearest and dearest rapes him on my dance floor, don't you?'

Will turned to the dance floor and laughed as Guido continued to struggle to constantly reposition Mel's octopus-like hand movements, which were at that moment trying to simultaneously squeeze his bum and grab his crotch as she sniggered away like an embarrassed teen.

'It's like watching a bear covered in honey trying to fend off a swarm of angry bees, how long have they been dancing like that?'

Dave smiled at Will's description.

'Oh, this is their fourth dance, we've had Kylie's *Spinning Around*, Candy Stanton's *Young Hearts* and Karl Douglas's *Kung-Fu Fighting* before this...but all with this same dance, it's like watching a weird new kind of reverse-tango-slash-car accident, all the same sweetheart, we should save the poor boy before he suffers some kind of deep psychological trauma which means he can't look at a French bob again without breaking into a cold sweat.'

Will patted Dave on the arm.

'I'll go, Dave, it's my round, mate, better get the drinks ready though as they may both be a bit over-emotional after that display!'.

Will could see the expression of relief growing on Guido's face as he approached, he smiled and nodded at him from behind Mel's back and then tapped her on the shoulder.

Her head flicked around quickly and she staggered as her body did its best to perform a one-eighty and follow her head. Will managed to catch her before she fell.

'Yaaay! It's my gorgeoushhhunhkymaan! ... Gissa smog, song, snog! Hee, hee!'

'Lovely to see you too, honey, come on, Mel, let's go and sit down over there, we can have a snog then, eh?'

Will propelled Mel towards the seating area and mouthed

'*coffee*' to Dave who nodded and gave him a thumbs up signal.

Mel kept laughing and licking at Will's neck like a hungry cat as he steered her quickly to an empty sofa.

'Okay then, babes, let's get you comfy then we can have a quick coffee and get you back to the hotel.'

Mel screwed up her face.

'Yuck! Don wan yucky coffee...wan shex on the bheeech!'

Will laughed.

'I think it's a bit wet outside for that, honey, and if you mean the cocktail then I think you're all cocktailed out, babe, how about we get naked in a nice warm bed?'

'Ooh yesh pleash! ... I wanna fug you like mad!'

Mel hugged Will tighter and stuck her tongue deep into his mouth, her hands fumbling away in a vain attempt to undo his jeans.

Dave approached the table carrying a large mug of black coffee and raised an eyebrow at Will in amusement. He placed it quietly on the table and winked at Will before backing away and mouthing "call me" while miming with the universal telephone gesture of his thumb and pinky sticking out as he raised his hand to his ear.

Will nodded and gave him a thumbs up, unable to dis-engage his face from Mel's.

Dave turned and sighed as he looked towards the bar at Guido, his nervous looking boyfriend was now necking a large brandy in a wine glass, *my poor baby, he'll live though...and it will be wonderful comforting him tonight when we slip between the sheets!*

Chapter Seven

Detective Inspector Rob Winters rubbed his eyes as the computer screen on his desk began to blur in and out of his focus. He yawned then leant back and opened the bottom drawer of his desk and reached in for the chocolate bar sat on top of his stab vest.

He knew that eating at your work station was strictly prohibited, but that rule only applied when the chief was around, and at nine pm on a Monday the chief would be tucking into dinner or plonked in front of the telly with the wife.

That meant he was the senior officer on duty till the shift change in an hour, so he could please himself.

He could see his reflection in the darker areas of the flat screen terminal as he munched down on the treat and savoured the gooey texture of chocolate and caramel on his tongue, a ghost image reminding him he was breaking rules again, and he revelled in the sugar-rush badness of it. He could hear the words of his wife and his doctor echoing through his mind, *you're heading for an early heart attack or diabetes if you don't cut down on the junk food old bean...* While his wife would be saying *you're in your fifties now, Rob, I don't want to be a widow in my fifties Rob...Rob? Are you listening to me, Rob? You are sooo selfish! You never listen, you just don't care about me or my feelings...*

'Fuck em all!' Rob looked around the office to see if anyone had heard but the other two officers were sat together, lost in concentration as they imagined themselves officers in the episode of C.S.I. Miami, or was it C.S.I. New York?

Rob couldn't see the screen clearly enough from his desk.

He jumped slightly as the phone rang with the "external caller" light flashing across its green display screen and he muttered 'Who the fuck?' as he reached across the desk.

'D.I. Winters speaking, how can I help?'

'Hello, Robert, my friend, it ees Enrique...'

Rob looked at the two young officers who had now turned to look at him, hopeful for a shout, a juicy murder...or bank robbery...with hostages, would be cool, then they could get tooled up and go in shooting, taking out bad guys and saving the day...Kapow! Kablammo!

Rob waved them away and shook his head and they turned around to lose themselves again in the glamorous law-enforcement, wet-dream world of American TV cops.

He disguised the nervousness he was feeling and went into his confident mode.

'Hello, Father, how nice to hear from you, everything okay at Saint Francis?'

'Yes, my friend, but there ees a young parishioner of mine I need to discuss with you, I am worried about hees spiritual health, can you come to see me after work this evening?'

Rob tried to maintain the lightness of his tone and disguise his stress despite the tightness of his chest and nausea he could feel rising in his throat

'Of course, Father, I'll be with you in thirty minutes. I just have to finish up here first.'

'Good, good, Robert. I look forward to seeing you, goodbye.'

Rob replaced the phone in its cradle and turned his attention to typing up his handover notes for the night shift senior officer.

He finished them after ten minutes then e-mailed them to the night shift, shut the computer off then rose to address the two officers.

'Andy, Tom, I'm off to meet a contact, I'll have my mobile in case we get a shout, unlikely though that is and I've e-mailed the handover to Jackie and the vampires. Keep it real guys! See you tomorrow lunchtime.'

The officers responded with the standard chorus of 'cheers guv' and 'have a good un!' as Rob strode quickly through the office.

He hated the hold that Fernandez had over him and thought back to the events of five years ago that had led to him being trapped in the web of this monster masquerading as a priest.

Rob had just turned forty five and was definitely going through the male menopause. He had just bought a shiny red Ducati 900cc motorbike and was using it one evening to follow up a lead from a local grass on where the sudden influx of crystal meth into Seafordby was originating from.

The grass had directed him to a sleazy local ne'er-do-well called Bryce Heston.

Rob revved the bike as he pulled up in the car park of The Venture Inn, a scruffy and ugly looking red brick bungalow at the rougher edge of Seafordby and well-known hang-out of the local criminal set.

He cut the engine and lifted his six-foot frame off the bike, his beer gut straining and creaking against the constraints of his brand new one-piece leathers. He removed his helmet and looked towards the pub, smiling as the two lookouts extinguished their spliffs and practically ran into the pub to warn everyone that "the filth are outside!".

He knew that this would prompt a mass exodus out the back of the pub but he wasn't worried about that. He had come to see the landlord, Dean Hambling, a pox-faced whale of a man-mountain and ex-con who made his money on kickbacks from drug dealers and selling knock off gear. He was also slippery as an eel and would be on the mobile to his lawyer moaning about "police harassment" before Rob had even stepped through the door.

He headed into the pub, running one hand over his bald pate to wipe away the beads of sweat that were forming there and gripped his crash helmet with his other massive paw, ready to use it as a weapon should the need arise.

He surveyed the dark smoke-filled interior of the pub, now

with just a smattering of a dozen customers, mostly male although a few rough-looking females scowled and shuffled closer to their protectors. Heavy Drum and Bass pumped out from a sound system in the corner controlled by a skinny pale DJ who had a set of headphones clutched to one ear as he leapt around behind the mixing decks, completely oblivious to all around him.

Rob smiled and approached the angry-looking landlord who seemed to have been lifted behind the bar by an industrial crane and wedged into place. Hambling growled and leaned forward with two club-like fists supporting his lamp-post-thick tattooed arms.

'Evening, Dean, is that cannabis I can smell or is it your new aftershave?'

'What the fuck do you want, cunt-stable? My lawyer's on his way already so make it quick, you know I'm allergic to pork and you stink of it Winters. Besides, you're scaring away my custom with your gay biker outfit.'

Hambling's acne scarred face broke into an ugly leer as he revealed his broken and blackened excuses for teeth.

Rob thumped the crash helmet down heavily on the wooden counter.

'Chill, fat boy, I'm not after you, I was wondering if you knew who Bryce was hanging out with these days?'

The landlord snorted derisively, 'Heston? That skinny rat fucker hasn't been in for weeks, he owes me a pony if you catch up with him.'

'I'll mention it to him, tell you what, Dean, you tell me what rock he's crawled under and I promise not to make this place the favoured after-work drinking hole of my colleagues and I for the next six months?'

Another snort from Hambling, 'Yeah right... I can just see you loving that. Try Fairfield Road, I heard he has a flat up there somewhere with some tart.'

Rob smiled at the gross landlord and picked his helmet up from the bar.

'Cheers, Dean, thanks for the info, you've been most helpful. Keep up with the beauty regimen, although I'd see someone about those botox injections, I think you got stiffed there, mate.' He made sure that everyone in the pub heard this last statement as he knew it would hurt Dean to have it put about that he co-operated with the Old Bill. He could see the anger rising as Dean's face turned a few shades closer to beetroot.

'Very funny, now fuck off out of my pub, filth!'

Rob pulled the Ducati to a stop outside of a small terraced house in Fairfield Road. He had phoned the station from the pub car park to check on known or recent offenders living in the street. There were a number of hits for residents with previous, but one stuck out in Rob's mind. A twenty-year-old woman cautioned for soliciting two weeks ago, first offence. It had Bryce Heston's stamp all over it. Hook up with a younger girl, then get her hooked, then get her hooking. Then get shot and move on when you'd milked the cash cow dry.

The street was a mixture of scruffy and well-looked-after houses. The property he was interested in definitely came down on the side of needing some attention.

Rob approached the white UPVC mock Victorian period door and rang the bell.

He rang it twice more before he heard a young woman's voice asking him to hold on. A light came on the hall and he could hear her breathing from the other side as she pushed her eye to the peep-hole viewer. Then he heard heavy bolts being thrown and a chain being put on the door before it was opened two inches and a curly blond perm was followed by bleary but pretty turquoise-blue eye peering around the gap.

'Are you Mike?'

Rob smiled, 'Mike?'

'My nine-thirty, you're half an hour late?'

Rob clicked, the client had obviously bottled out.

'Ohh, yeah that's right. Your nine-thirty, yeah sorry I got held up,' he grinned nervously at the pretty half-face.

'Hold on I'll get the door.'

There was a further throwing of bolts before the door was pulled open.

'Come on in, love, close the door and do the bolts for me would ya? We're in the back room. Second door on your right.'

Rob watched as the barefoot girl trudged away from him wearing nothing but a large U2 T-shirt that didn't quite cover her lacy pink knickers, that didn't quite cover her Kylie Minogue-shaped behind.

Rob could feel his heart rate increase. She was not Bryce's normal type at all. For starters she was really pretty, and she was blonde. Bryce seemed to go for plump brunettes or redheads that were a bit plain and a bit older than this girl.

He secured the door and walked along the corridor, taking a quick look in the front room as he passed. It was furnished with two cheap sofa's, cheap beige carpet, a cheaper coffee table, complete with empty sweet wrappers, crisp packets and stained coffee mugs.

A large widescreen telly sat in the fireplace, but no sign of Bryce.

He continued down the corridor to the back room and pushed open the door.

The girl was sat on a large double bed with red pillows. A red scarf covering a lamp that stood on the bedside cabinet. The only other items in the room were a chest of drawers and a long book shelf on one wall with a large collection of tired-looking paper-backs heaped up higgledy-piggledy.

'Hey, Mike ...I like your leathers, are you a biker then?'

The girl smiled at Rob revealing a set of perfect white teeth behind her full red lips.

'Err, yeah that's right...sorry I can't remember your name? What was it again?'

'It's Donna, but you can call me whatever you like, darling, you sounded different on the phone, older, and you had more of an accent.'

Rob thought quickly, this girl was unsettling him.

'Oh that, well I like to disguise my voice, you know for security and that.' *You knob! Security, where did you drag that up from dickhead?*

'Oh right, well like I said on the phone, straight sex with a blow job is eighty quid, double it if you want anal and you get half an hour. If you want longer or anything kinky we can negotiate a price.'

'Erm how about the one hundred and sixty quid package then?'

Rob could feel himself sweating underneath the leathers. *What the hell are you playing at? You're supposed to be after Bryce, you're a fucking police inspector and this girl is a victim, what about Maggie?*

Rob couldn't remember the last time he had been intimate with his wife, two years ago? On holiday in Portugal. It had been disappointing for both of them. Too much cheap wine and a heavy meal hadn't helped things along. But this girl, this young beautiful girl was turning him on and he could already feel his cock swelling against the leather trousers. Besides, if she said anything it would be her word against his, and she may provide a lead on Bryce. It couldn't hurt, just this once. He knew he had already justified it in his mind and he was ready to worry about the consequences later on.

Donna smiled and held an open palm towards him.

'Cash up front then, Mister big spender'

Twenty minutes later Rob positioned his rock hard cock at the opening of her anus. She lubed the opening and put extra lube on the condom covering Rob's shaft.

Rob was breathing hard as she guided his cock into her rectum, giving loud moans as he pushed further into her hole. He gasped at the tightness and how he could feel her fingers through the wall of her vagina as she played with herself.

He pushed deeper and increased his rhythm as her moans became louder and louder. He knew he was going to come soon, so he sped up as her moans and shouts increased in volume.

'Yeah! That's it! That's it darlin'! Fuck my arsehole, oooh! You dirty bastard! Fuck my dirty bum-hole! Yes! Yes! Fuck my arse! Fuck my arse!'

Rob let out a loud cry as he let go, feeling his semen gush out inside her.

He pulled out quickly and collapsed next to her on the bed, gasping for air and sweating.

'Shit!..I'm getting too old for this…'

Donna giggled and patted him on the chest.

'You did okay, Mike, I've had worse darling, a lot worse, and they were much younger than you!'

Rob looked at Donna and felt like crying. This young, damaged victim was reassuring him, talking to him as though he were a bashful schoolboy. A man old enough to be her father, a man who had abused his position and was with her under false pretences. He felt the shame, self-loathing and guilt welling up inside him like a thunderstorm. Ready to break on the hillside and weep floods of rain onto a waiting silent valley below. He felt his body begin to shake and sat up in the bed, leaning forwards to place his head in his hands and he began to cry as he had never cried before.

The next thing he knew, Donna was cradling him in her small soft arms, holding his head to her breasts and making soothing noises.

'Hey now…shhhh, it's okay…shhhh.' It only made him feel even more of a total shit.

After he had recovered and dressed back into the leathers he was able to bring himself to ask about Bryce.

'So, err...do you have a boyfriend then, Donna?'

The young girl seemed completely unaffected by his emotional outburst and was sat up on the bed with her knees drawn up to her chest and the T-shirt pulled down over them, only her feet and shocking pink painted toenails stuck out at the bottom. She took a pull on her cigarette and smiled shyly at Rob.

'Yeah, I've got a fellah.'

'And does he mind you doing this?'

She shrugged and looked down at her toes, rocking her body forwards and then back slightly. Now she looked vulnerable and sad, like a broken porcelain doll. He wanted to sweep her up and carry her away with him to safety but he knew that would ruin everything. He would bide his time and rescue her later, when he made a plan. Take her away from all the abuse and hurt.

'He looks after me...makes sure I'm sorted, he keeps the weirdo's away.'

All the earlier bravado and confidence had left her voice as she squeaked out excuses for her pimp.

'He sounds nice, Bryce isn't it?'

She jumped slightly as Rob mentioned the name. She stared up at Rob, now curious and cautious.

'Yeah that's right, you know him do you?'

Rob threw her a reassuring smile, 'Sure...everyone knows Bryce, he's a dude.'

She relaxed a bit and went back to smoking her cigarette.

'Yeah he's a cool guy.'

'So then, Donna, can I see you again sometime?' Rob continued smiling at her. Donna shrugged again.

'Whatever...'

'Great! Oh, I lost the bit of paper I had your mobile number on and I was calling from a mate's house earlier, what was it again?'

Donna got up from the bed and pulled open the bottom drawer in the chest. She scrabbled around until she found a pen and then she flattened out a crumpled piece of paper, her tongue sticking out as she concentrated on writing the figures in her best hand. It made her look even younger than her twenty years and Rob felt that pang again in the pit of stomach, desire mixed with guilt and shame.

She skipped over to him, delighted with her work, the student seeking approval of the teacher, presenting the piece of paper to him as though she were handing over the complete works of Shakespeare.

Rob looked at the paper and beamed at Donna. She had written her name in block capitals under the number, and drawn a little smiley face in the "O" of "DONNA".

'Wow! You've got lovely handwriting, thanks, Donna.'

She smiled proudly as he leaned forward to kiss her on the cheek.

'Thanks, darling, don't leave it too long before coming to see me again, I kinda like you, Mister big softie biker!'

'Don't, worry baby, you'll be seeing me soon'. Rob grinned and picked up his crash helmet from next to the bedroom door. Donna followed him to the front door and threw her arms around him as he turned to say goodbye, planting a wet kiss on his lips.

'Bye, softie biker Mike.'

Rob broke her embrace and turned to open the door.

'Bye, sexy Donna, I'll be in touch soon, I promise.'

Rob saw more and more of Donna over the next month. His chief had asked about how the investigation was progressing as he seemed to be spending a lot of time out of the office. Rob had reassured him that he was on the verge of breaking the case but things were at a crucial stage with his inside contact.

In reality he hadn't mentioned Bryce to Donna since their first meeting except to make sure that her "boyfriend" was not around whenever he phoned to arrange a session with her. He had more or less forgotten about his original purpose for visiting Donna, completely smitten with the young girl as he was.

This fact didn't help ease his sense of panic when he received a mysterious phone call from the recently appointed priest of Saint Francis Parish, asking to meet him to discuss Donna.

How did he know about Donna? More to the point how much did he know about Donna and him?

Rob was trying to stay calm as he sat in the plush, warm office of Father Fernandez. He had been waiting for ten minutes and was getting edgy and angry with this upstart newcomer to his patch. He had already met Fernandez six months ago, when the outgoing priest had brought him to the District Community Forum to introduce him to the great and the good that watched over the moral health and status quo of the people of Seafordby.

Rob had simply shook his hand and made the correct interested noises when he was introduced to the Spaniard. The only thing he could remember thinking was that he was a bit too smooth and good-looking to be a priest, but had otherwise instantly forgotten about the man.

The door swung open and Rob got up from his seat as Fernandez swept into the room.

'Good evening, Eenspector Winters, may I call you Robert? Thank you for coming so promptly.'

The two men shook hands. Rob was surprised by the firmness of the priest's grip.

'Of course, Father, how can I be of assistance?'

Fernandez smiled and released Rob's hand.

'Please, Robert, call me Enrique, we are both professional men yes?'

'Certainly, Enrique, how do you know Donna Thompson?'

'Ahh, the lovely Donna! We will come to that shortly, firstly may I offer you a seengle malt Whiskey?'

'That's very kind of you, thank you.'

Fernandez talked over his shoulder as he busied himself in preparing the drinks.

'I expect you have many questions in your head, Robert. Please do not worry, I will answer them all soon. You asked how you could assist me but eet ees I who will assist you, Robert. I am aware of many things that you are not.'

Fernandez turned and handed the large tumbler to Rob.

'Please follow me, Robert, bring your drink. You may need eet.'

Rob followed the priest along the vaulted corridor to a heavy wooden door which the priest unlocked with a large old-fashioned key. They immediately entered a dimly lit landing at the top of stone steps that spiralled away beneath them. Fernandez locked the door behind Robert and led him down the steps until they reached another heavy wooden door which the priest used the same key to open and then lock behind them.

Robert looked around at the dimly lit corridor. It seemed to mirror exactly the corridor above but the stone was much darker. He could smell damp, and a musty, ancient odour of candles and incense permeated from the stones. This place definitely had age, then another rusty smell that he recognised all too well filled his nostrils. The distinctive stink of the abattoir and morgue, blood.

The place reeked of it and Rob felt a shiver run through him as pearls of cold sweat ran down his back. He took a large gulp from the tumbler, pausing to inhale the sweet, peaty aroma of the whiskey in an attempt to block out the rank smell of the cellar.

'My apologies, Robert, I am used to the smell so I forget how bad eet ees. I should have warned you. This way, my friend, I have something to show you that I know will interest you.'

Rob followed the man along the corridor to another solid door, this one was padded with some kind of foam around the frame and as soon as the priest opened the door Rob's ears were assaulted by Ricky Martin's *La Vida Loca* playing at maximum volume.

What he saw caused him to vomit on the spot.

What remained of Bryce Heston was strapped to a solid wooden chair at one end of the room.

Both his hands were missing and bloody cauterized stumps punctuated his arms. Two gaping bloody holes stared out at Rob in place of Bryce's eyes and his body was covered in burns and deep gouges where large lumps of flesh had been removed. Rob only recognised him from the large black Chinese dragon tattoo that stretched from shoulder to shoulder across his torso. The mutilation of his body made the dragon look as though it was melting down his chest and the policeman knew that Bryce had died slowly and probably very painfully. He felt as though his heart was being squeezed in a vice and shook his head slowly as he surveyed the area immediately in front of body which was strewn with fingers, toes, chunks of flesh and Bryce's severed genitalia. Suddenly the music stopped and Rob snapped out of his shock to stare at Fernandez as he stood at a large heavy workbench covered in bloodstained metal tools and D.I.Y. equipment.

He recovered himself and wiped the flecks of vomit from the corners of his mouth, quickly downed the rest of his tumbler, before shouting at the priest.

'You sick twisted fucker! You are so fucking nicked!'

Fernandez held up a hand to silence Rob.

'Please control yourself, Robert! I need you to watch this.'

The priest switched on a bulky old television that was sat at one end of the workbench and pushed a silver DVD into the slot underneath the screen, hitting the play button as he did so.

Rob stepped forward to get a better view of the images on the screen and he knew immediately what he was seeing. He had fallen for the oldest trick in the book and felt sick at having been trapped so easily, so completely. He watched in resigned self-disgust as the image of a naked Donna entering the room, smiling and leading a naked Robert Winters by his erect cock towards the bed, filled the television screen. This was from their session last week and he felt his legs turn to jelly underneath him. *The bookshelf, it was so fucking obvious! Why hadn't he checked the bookshelf!*

'Enough! ... Please! Switch it off! ... I've seen enough.'

Fernandez hit the stop button and turned to face Rob.

'I am sorry that I had to show you this, Robert my friend. There are several more DVDs I have obtained from the sorry excuse for a man that now sits in that chair. Eet will comfort you to know that Donna had no knowledge of Meester Heston's little habit of filming her with her...customers. He was planning to blackmail you of course, but first he came to me...you see Meester Heston had a business arrangement with me and he owed me a large amount of money. He had approached me three months ago and asked me to fund a business venture he had planned. When he was unable to make a repayment, he tried to offer this filth to me! So now you understand Robert, you understand why I call you...yes?

I will give all of these "home movies" to you of course, my friend. But as you can see, I have a business venture that involves...how can I say this? Unusual methods...yes, bueno, unusual methods.'

The priest placed a comforting hand on Rob's shoulder.

'Come, my friend, let us go back upstairs to my office where your senses can be recovered yes?'

Rob felt numb and broken as he allowed the priest to lead him out of the cellar and the horror it contained.

After his second tumbler of alcohol Rob had recovered himself enough to know that this priest now owned him. He sighed and looked up from the armchair at Fernandez who was leaning on the stone fireplace surround and staring into the flames of the fire.

'So then, Enrique, what happens now?'

Fernandez turned to Rob and smiled gently.

'Nothing, my friend, I have rid you of your problems with this man. He was a drug-dealer and vile whore-master, a corrupter of innocents and I have sent hees poisoned soul to burn in the flames of Hell for all eternity. He will not be missed by society and certainly not by law enforcement officials such as yourself? His death also means that your young girlfriend ees free. You can be with her exclusively now, this ees what you wanted yes? ... As for me, I only will ask a small service of you.'

*Here it comes...*thought Rob.

'And what service would that be?'

Fernandez moved to the desk and relaxed back into his comfortable leather chair, resting his elbows on the arm supports, he steepled his hands together and brought them to his chin. He shrugged.

'I only ask for your silence about my business activities, that ees not so difficult I think, yes? Also I may need to come to you for information on those that I do business with in the future. As you can see my friend, I have dealings with many people who are known to the authorities in some way. All that I am looking for ees...how do you say? ... The competition's edge? In return for this information, I offer you my silence, friendship and protection, also I will give you the video evidence that ees so painful and damaging to you. Are we in agreement, Robert?'

Robert felt the wave of nausea rise in him again. He knew that what he should do is arrest this sick fuck and let him rot in jail forever, God only knew how many poor individuals this twisted sadist had dispatched in the torture chamber below his feet. He also realised that nicking this madman would mean losing his job, his wife and any hope of a future with Donna and Rob's brain reasoned that in his own sick way, the priests activities had rid the town of a major scum-bag in Bryce Heston, the case was definitely closed on that one, and the chances were he would continue to thin out the undesirable elements of Seafordby and the surrounding area, thereby make Rob's job a hell of a lot easier. Rob suddenly felt overwhelmed and exhausted by the whole experience. He nodded slowly before looking up at Fernandez.

'Okay, Enrique, I agree.'

Five years on and Rob was sat in the now familiar office. He detested this man with every fibre of his being and thought about the countless fantasies he had dreamt up about killing Fernandez in the same way that he had disposed of his victims. At the same time he recognised that if the truth were ever to emerge about the gruesome goings-on in the cellar of the church then he would be left with no alternative but suicide. He knew that the sick bastard was bound to have made copies of the sex DVDs of Donna and himself.

He did his best to hide his anger and revulsion.

'How can I help, Enrique?'

Fernandez pushed a sheet of paper across the table towards Rob.

'I am sorry to bother you once again, Robert, but I need to know any information that you have about this man, Will Cummings, and hees family. I believe he works at the Highcliff Hotel.'

Rob picked up the sheet of paper and read the details on it.

'His name rings a bell with me but I can't recollect why off the top of my head. I don't think he's a major player but I'll check him out on the database and get back to you tomorrow afternoon, is that soon enough for you?'

'That would be very kind of you, Robert, as ever, I am in your debt, my friend.'

The priest raised his glass in salute to Rob.

Rob forced a smile through his gritted teeth,

You mean I am the one who is forever in debt to you...you perverted shit!

Chapter Eight

Will stood on the balcony and punched the dial button for Luke on his mobile phone. He looked over his shoulder to the bed. Mel's face was turned towards him and the rest of her naked form was spread across the bed in a star shape, half-buried under the duvet. Her full red lips were slightly parted and a small trickle of saliva was running from the corner of her mouth to dampen the pillow. She looked childlike and peaceful.

She'll be out for the count for the rest of the night probably, time to get this plan rolling to stage two, thought Will.

He knew that he was taking some big risks with this plan and they could both wind up in jail, dead or...he suddenly recalled his meeting with Fernandez, making the hairs stand up on the back of his neck and a shiver run through his body. Maybe there were fates worse than death, but as Will looked at Mel he felt that ache in his heart and the butterflies in the pit of his stomach, and he knew that he would risk everything for her. Walk across hot coals, move mountains, beg, steal and borrow, go up against Fernandez and SUBDL.

Whatever it took, he was ready to do it.

The ringing stopped at the other end of the line and his mind snapped back into focus.

'Awl right, Will mate! How's tricks?'

'Al-right Luke? I'm fine, mate, look I need a favour, bro.'

'You know me, mate, I've got your back fellah, wotcher need?'

'I need a meet with Anton Golding, you still getting draw from him?'

'Err...maybe, mate, maybe, you're not in any trouble, bruv? I mean, you know contacting another player before a big match is strictly verboten by the league, so you're takin' a big risk mate. On second thoughts, don't tell me if you are in trouble as I don't want to fuckin' know, pal, then no fucker can chop me nads off tryin' to get it out of me eh?'

'Yeah I know, Luke, don't sweat it mate. If anyone asks me, this conversation never happened'.

'Well, I'm a bit busy, mate, I've just sent an email to Ralph Lauren complaining that "The Big Pony Club" infringes copyright on my "North London Big Pony's" web site which shows naked muscular men in the act of taking large poohs, it kind of validates my marketing strategy but totally misdirects my scat fan base, heh, heh…know wot I mean, dude?'

'Heh, Jeez, Luke…you are such a mucky arsehole mate, god knows how you fuckin' live with yourself, but I need an in with Anton.'

Will swallowed as he waited for his friends answer, Luke was the guy that got him through being inside, he owed him big time. The last thing he wanted to do was involve him with something that could get him killed, but he knew that if Luke said no, then he would have to go straight to Anton which would be a very risky move on his part. He needed Luke to arrange the meet, but hopefully he could minimise the risk to both of them.

'Look, mate, if I do this for you…and fuck knows why you want to put your bollocks on the block like this, then you owe me big time, and I mean big time! We cool bruv…?'

Will could feel his hand trembling as he held the phone to his ear.

'We're cool, Luke, and if you ever need payback for this…you know I'll be there, bruv.'

'Good, good. We're straight on that then, bro, when and where do you need this to happen?'

Will thought quickly, he needed to get to London, go to Mel's and then do the meet, then get back to Seafordby for the nine pm meet with Fernandez to sign for the money. It would have to be somewhere near Mel's place in Camden, and somewhere where the eyes and ears of SUBDL were unlikely to be. He suddenly had an idea, there was a favourite Sunday hangout for him and his student mates.

'Crystal Palace park in Penge , near the Concert Bowl, ask him to meet you there at two pm tomorrow, by the statue of Dante.'

'Fuck me, Will, you don't want much do ya...fuckin' hell!'

There was a long pause as Luke thought it over.

'Alright, mate, I'll see wot I can do, if the venue changes I'll let you know, mate...you must 'ave some kinda death wish though bruvver! I'll be in touch, dude.'

'Cheers, Luke, catch you later, mate.'

Will hit the end call button and then searched his contacts for Dave's number, he pushed the button and waited. It was going to be a busy few days.

Mel opened a watery eye as daylight streamed into the room, she moaned and pulled the duvet up and over her pounding head. The bitter aroma of fresh coffee, along with the smell of cooked bacon, filled her nostrils.

Will gave a little laugh,

'Morning, sweetheart, bit of a sore head today?'

'Ngrrahhhh...'

'Wow! I think that's a whole new language you've just invented, honey, a simple yes would do...here, drink this.'

Will passed his hand free hand under the duvet and found one of Mel's hands, then he slid the glass of fizzing clear liquid into the waiting fingers. Mel grunted,

'Wottisssit?'

'Just drink it, Mel, you'll feel a lot better honest.'

Will was doing his best not to laugh but the humour in his tone was difficult to hide.

'Mmkhay.'

Mel drank the liquid while still under the duvet, it did revive her a bit as her mouth felt as though it was full of sawdust before drinking it.

'Tastes yucky...whattimeissit?'

Will leaned over from his position on the bed and gently lifted the duvet away from Mel's shoulder, planting a soft kiss there as he did so.

'It's seven-thirty, honey, but we've got a big day today. Do you think you can manage some fresh coffee and a hot bacon roll? I managed to head down to the kitchen and beg some brekkie from the chef.'

'Mmm...that's more like it...bring it on, baby,' murmured a sleepy Mel.

Thirty minutes later their naked bodies were intertwined in the stream of the power-shower.

Mel felt the hot sting of the water on her back and neck as the water mixed with their kisses.

Will's head moved down to her breast and he took an erect nipple into his mouth and bit gently on the hard pink nub while his free hand found its way between her thighs. She raised one leg slightly and re-positioned her hips to allow his hand easier access, gripping his shoulder with one hand as her other soaped his erection and ball sack. The sensation of prickly wet heat from the shower and Will's slippery body, combined with her frustrations from the previous night's fumbling with Guido were driving her rapidly to a frenzy. She pulled Will closer and guided his cock into her hot wet hole. It was as though she was on fire and was desperate to burn like a collapsing sun, craving the heat and hardness of Will's body.

Will felt her urgency and passion, he lifted her legs and supported her body pushing back against the tiled wall of the shower as they began to move together, thrusting and grinding against each other.

Mel felt as if she were a wild animal that wanted to consume Will completely, as her heat and passion rose she could feel the wave of her orgasm growing. She bit down hard on Will's shoulder as she clung to his body and they both cried out loudly as her legs began to shake from the earthquake starting deep inside her. Mel closed her eyes as Will's body seemed to turn to burning rock and she could feel the hot liquid of his orgasm jetting deep inside her.

White sparks of light danced inside the back of closed eyelids and she felt as though she was floating higher and higher above the clouds.

As they clung tightly together, the hot water streaming over their still shaking bodies, the intense emotion overpowering, Mel opened her eyes and looked at Will. It was then that she realised they were both crying.

And it was then, as she felt her chest tighten with a longing and sadness that felt unbearable, she knew how deeply she was in love with him.

Will reached up and turned off the shower, they kissed the tears and the water from each other's faces.

'Explain it to me again, why do you have to go to London today and on Friday?'

Mel sat on the bed in a white towelling robe, drying her hair furiously with a small hotel towel.

Will was throwing clothing and objects quickly into his Gola holdall.

'I've told you, babe, it's a league meeting and I've got to go, I'll be back tonight and Dave is taking you out for the day, you'll have a blast, honey.'

Mel suddenly stopped her frantic rubbing and looked angrily at Will.

'I seriously hope you are not planning to interfere with my..."situation", Will? You made a promise to me and believe me, I will be able to put my feelings for you to one side and ditch you if interfere...as well as bloody killing you!'

Will walked over to where Mel was sitting on the bed and placed his hands on her shoulders, a serious and sad expression on his face.

'Much as I want to interfere, I made a promise to you, Mel, and this is just a league meeting. I'll get back as soon as possible.'

Mel smiled sadly at Will and leaned forward, pressing her head to his stomach as she wrapped her arms around his midriff.

'Okay, baby, I'm just a bit paranoid about this whole thing, sorry. Just be careful and hurry back, okay?'

Will leaned down kissed the top of her head.

'Received and understood sweets. By the way, you need me to pick up anything from yours? ... Seeing as I'm gonna be in the neighbourhood.'

Mel broke her hold and looked up excitedly

'Ooohhh, yes! I forgot to pack my GHDs, silly cow that I am...and you can pick up some clothes. I'll make a list, that would be fab!'

'No problem, honey.'

Will had been banking on Mel needing something from the flat, it would save him the problem of lifting her keys, which would arouse her suspicions if she noticed them missing.

Mel jumped up from the bed and danced over to her bag on the dressing table, fishing around for the keys. There was a knock on the door and Will crossed the room and pulled the door open to reveal a smiling Dave.

'Morning, campers! How are my little Paris and Helen of Troy this morning then?'

He pecked Will on the cheek and skipped past him and on to Mel who was now sat scribbling instructions on a piece of hotel paper. Dave leaned over and gave her a huge hug, repeating the kiss on the cheek and then resting his head on her shoulder as they both grinned at their reflections in the mirror.

'We are going to have such a girlie day of pampering, dahling! Now finishing with the scribblings pleases! And we'll get rid of your fella and get ready for some quality lady fun!!'

Mel laughed and reached up to touch Dave's hand affectionately.

'Dave, you're amazing, you could cheer up corpses in bloody morgue!'

Dave screwed his face up.

'Ughh, no ta, dearie! I prefer a bit of life in my audience. Now let's start with getting you looking mind-blowingly glamorous!'

Will shook his head and smiled at the scene as he pushed the door closed and crossed to the dressing table.

'I can see you two are gonna have fun today.'

Anton Golding tapped one leg nervously on the ground as he sat on the park bench. He had a clear view of the statue of Dante from where he was and could see Derek, his lookout for today, the far side of the bust, leaning against a tree as he played with his mobile phone. He checked his gold Tag Huer watch.

1.55, Luke be here soon, him better have a good deal for I, or I be fuckin' that little runt up, big style.

He glanced around to his left and then to right side. That was when he saw Will walking towards him with a bulging red holdall,

Oh ras man. This could be trouble.

He smiled at Will and started to shake his head, turning to look down at his size-twelve Converse All-stars.

Will sat down on the bench next to Anton. He was puffing and out of breath as he had just done a perimeter check of the park for any SUBDL faces. Also it had taken him longer than he thought to find Mel's passport in the flat, which was a lot messier than he'd expected.

'Hello, Anton mate, long time no see'

Anton turned to look at Will, an expression of resigned disappointment on his face.

'Man, you tryin ta get I and I killed? And don't fuckin "mate" me, fact you sat here means you ain't me friend.'

'Sorry about this Anton but just hear me out, I'm in big trouble and I need your help.'

Anton listened patiently and with interest as Will ran through the events of the last couple of weeks. He put a large hand up and stroked his soul patch thoughtfully.

'So, what exactly it you need from I, bro?'

'I've got ten grand here and two passports, hers and mine. I'll need two new passports with different names, but they've got to be good, well, good enough to get us out of the country anyway, plus I'll throw the match on Friday.'

Anton gave a loud laugh and slapped his thigh.

'You funny, mon! What make you think me not gonna whip you anyway?'

Will gave a quick shrug of his shoulders.

'Maybe, but I can make sure I have an "off day" so it's guaranteed, you could make quite a bit of folding on the strength of that, if you lay the bets off carefully enough.'

Anton was deep in thought for a while as he weighed up the risks and possibilities.

'The money will easy cover costs on the passports, me be taking a big risk with the bets, but it nothing me can't cope with...then again, me may just tell SUBDL about our likkle meeting, you get a few missing fingers, and me get ten grand richer, how that sound, bro? You a crazy fool ya'know...but me can appreciate what love do a body, so good luck to you both. See me cuz over by the tree there?'

Will looked over to where Derek was still playing absently with the phone and glancing around from time to time. He nodded.

'Him called Derek, a bit slow, but him a good boy, sharp-eyed. Him meet you after the game on Friday at Paddington and hand over the passports. You won't check him, him come find you, so don't worry 'bout phone call or nothing. You just find somewhere to stand and him soon come, alright?'

Will looked at Anton, he knew that Anton might not have been joking about telling SUBDL but he had to take big risks all round now. He reached down and unzipped the bag, took out a bulging white envelope and passed it to Anton.

'Thanks, Anton, I won't forget this.'

He offered his hand to Anton and the big man clasped his hand in a firm grip.

'You alright, bro, me miss playin' against you. You take care now, and take care of that woman of yours. Me see you Friday'

They both stood up and Anton broke into a big smile, he turned away, signalled to Derek to follow and shook his head laughing and saying 'Rare ting' to himself as he walked away from Will.

Will headed in the opposite direction and was grim-faced, he couldn't have felt less like laughing in his life. He had crossed the line now and there was definitely no turning back from here.

Detective Inspector Winters yawned and stretched as he sat in an unmarked Mitsubishi Evo, eyed the middle-aged skinhead with the beer belly as he left the amusement arcade and moved towards a silver Mercedes S-Class. He had been following this fat wanker around for the last two hours, and the man had done absolutely nothing that even smacked of illegality. He reached across into the glove compartment and pulled out his spare mobile phone that he kept for what he liked to call, "extra-curricular" activity, switched it on, and punched in the speed dial for Fernandez's number.

'Hello, my friend, you have some news for me, yes?'

Rob winced as he heard that heavy accent, how he hated that voice. He would often hear it in his nightmares, laughing and mocking him, and he would wake sweating, gasping for breath and clutching his chest.

He swallowed and flicked his notebook open to the last entry.

'Yes, Father, our mutual friend was a bit of a naughty boy a few years back. He got three years for possession of a class-A substance with intent to supply, of which he served eighteen months. He's been down here and working in various bar jobs for the past three years, has been at the hotel for just over a year. His intelligence report shows that he deals a small amount of weed, the odd bit of ecstasy and mandy, sorry Father...MDMA, but nothing like what he was doing in London. He makes regular trips to and from the capital about once every month or so, presumably to score but we're not sure on that one. Apart from that, he's got a couple of arrests for drunk and disorderly, but he's strictly small time and so not of any interest to us at the moment. His family check out as clean. No brothers or sisters, parents live in Chippenham, but not so much as a parking ticket on them. That's all I can give you on him, Enrique.'

'No, no, Robert, you have been more than thorough as usual. Thank you, my friend. I look forward to our next meeting.'

The phone went dead at the other end.

Robert held the handset away from him with disgust, then threw it back into the glove-box before starting the engine and pulling out into the traffic to follow the Mercedes.

'Yeah, fuck you too, ya cunt.'

Fernandez put the phone down on the desk and turned his attention back to the Sony Vaio laptop and his sermon for this Sunday. He knew how Winters must hate him, and that was why he liked to summon the police inspector every now and again. It proved to Fernandez that he held all the cards, plus he liked to see Winters to better gauge the policeman's state of mind. He firmly believed that his police source would be dead within a year, *probably from a heart attack while screwing his young mistress,* thought Fernandez.

At least Winters had confirmed his suspicions about Will Cummings. The young man had obviously decided to join the bigger players in the local drug market, he would transfer the funds to Cummings account later that evening. Fernandez returned his thoughts to his sermon, he thought "The Wages of

Sin" would be an apt topic for this week's lecture. Not that he normally delivered it to a more than half-empty church.

He smiled to himself as he secretly fantasised about what he would do if Mr Cummings failed to meet the repayments.

Yes, the wages of sin are indeed death, and for my new young friend, a very long and painful one possibly.

Chapter Nine

Will sat in the priest's study at exactly nine pm, as they had agreed.

He had received a text from Dave earlier that evening as he was heading back from London. Dave said that they were having "theatrical and movie theme evening at the club" and informed Will that Fernandez's money was now safely in the Blue Lagoon account as they had discussed. Dave had previously offered this to Will as an option, as such a large sum of money would attract attention if it went straight into Will's bank account, but it would not even raise an eyebrow by going through Dave's business account for the club.

If Saint Francis church gave him the creeps before, it seemed positively nightmarish now as he sat waiting for Fernandez. He felt absolutely exhausted and mentally drained after spending the last thirteen hours in travelling, searching Mel's apartment and secret meetings.

He turned in his chair as he heard the heavy oak-panelled door open behind him.

'Ahh, young Meester Cummings, my apologies for keeping you waiting. I trust all ees well with you, my friend?'

The tall Spaniard moved quickly towards Will, his large hand thrust forward in welcome. Will rose to shake hands,

'Yes thanks, Father, I'm a bit tired though, had a busy day'

Fernandez moved to the filing cabinet next to the desk and motioned for Will to sit down. He pulled open the top drawer and removed a hanging folder that was tagged with Will's name. He moved opposite Will and opened the file on the desk, removed a letter and pushed the paper across the plush leather table top.

'Of course, of course, please sit and be comfortable, this formality will not take us long. I have merely to obtain your signature on thees letter and we will have agreement.'

Will studied the letter which stated that he had received the eighty thousand pounds and was signing to acknowledge receipt.

Fernandez gave a slight cruel smile as Will read the letter.

'I took the liberty of transferring the funds to the account number you gave me over two hours ago, but please my friend, feel free to confirm thees if you wish.'

Will looked up at Fernandez and returned the priests smile.

'It's okay, Father, I've already had it confirmed thanks'

'Bueno! Then you have only to sign and our business for thees evening ees concluded.'

He reached into his desk and offered Will the Mont Blanc pen.

Will took the pen and signed the document hurriedly, then handed the pen and paper back to Fernandez.

'Excellent, my young friend! Now I must insist that you go home and get some rest, you must remain healthy, yes? We must feed the body as well as the soul my friend, and you do seem a little tired. I will see you for the repayment as you have agreed in your form, yes?'

Will stood and offered his hand to the priest, he wanted to run as far away from this man as he could and fought hard to keep his composure.

'Err, yes…that's right, as we agreed, thanks, Father…bye.'

Fernandez took Will's hand and gripped it firmly, pulling Will towards him slightly so that he could look him closer in the eye and he made no attempt to hide the tone of malice in his voice.

'Good evening, Will, I look forward to our next meeting, very much indeed…now please excuse me if I do not escort you out, but I have many Parish matters to…attend to.'

Once Will had exited the office, he practically ran down the long gloomy corridor to the exit of the church. There was something about Fernandez that made Will feel nauseous and made his skin crawl.

He made his way to the beaten up old Peugeot and headed back to The Blue Lagoon, the weariness almost overwhelming him on the short drive.

Will couldn't help but laugh at the sight that greeted him as he entered the night club.

Sinister Dave was in a full silver-sequinned ball gown, complete with a massive blonde beehive wig and fake boobs doing his best 'Divine' impersonation. He was sat on a high-backed red armchair that had been converted to a throne with elaborate gold brocade trimming the edges of the chair. Guido was wearing a pair of skin-tight leopard-skin briefs, Chelsea boots and looked as if he had been dipped in oil and stood to one side of the throne with a large white feather fan which he was using to cool Dave down by wafting it at him. Meanwhile his "courtiers" consisted of Mel who was dressed as Sally Bowles from Cabaret (complete with bowler hat), Lucy and Jasmine, Dave's promotional assistants, were dressed as Barberella (complete with zap gun) and Lara Croft (complete with silver automatics).

They were gyrating suggestively against each other as the original club mix of 'Groovebird' by Natural Born Grooves blasted around the club. They were all drinking Tequila Sunrises in frosted cocktail glasses, and were being cheered on by a large crowd of revellers.

Will shook his head, laughing as he headed for the bar.

Only Dave could have dreamed up that little fantasy, genius, looks like it's gonna be a long night!

Mel woke first the following afternoon and threw on the towelling robe. Moving to the balcony she opened the French windows as quietly as she could and stepped out to light a cigarette. Her feet enjoying the cold stone. Her head was still fuzzy and the cigarette was making her feel light-headed. She watched as a watery sun headed towards the west end of the bay and had half disappeared over the headland.

Last night's party had gone on long after the club had shut when they had moved upstairs to Dave's apartment.

She had a blurred memory of lots of lines of coke, Viagra and eccys being done, and then the party turning into a major Roman orgy. She could remember Will entering her from behind as she had her face buried in Jasmines crotch, while Lucy played with his balls and sucked at her clitoris hungrily from underneath her. Dave was naked on the couch with Guido's head moving rapidly up down between Dave's thighs, but he was watching Will greedily. Then later as she was sucking at Guido's stiff cock, she watched as Jasmine fucked Dave with a strap-on, it looked almost comical, this tiny blonde riding this huge man and whooping "yee-hars" as Dave gasped beneath her. Then she had felt her legs tremble as Lucy, now minus her Barberella outfit, made her come, mouth moving feverishly between Mel's thighs and Lucy herself was moaning in-between the flicks of her tongue as Will thrust hard into her from the rear.

She felt a tingle between her legs as she recalled the sensations and pleasure of it all.

She also remembered that most of that had been her suggestion, and now felt pangs of guilt that she had been so out of control, and so wild.

Well, you said you wanted major party mayhem for these last two weeks and you certainly got that last night, girl, and some...nasty.

It was as though she was a desert flower dying of thirst in the arid climate, sucking hungrily at the earth, trying to extract every drop of moisture as it clung on desperately to its brief existence.

She felt more weary than she had ever felt in her life, the pressure of the world was crushing and overpowering, and she wanted this to be her last day, but knew there were four more days of this torture to endure. She turned and looked at Will's naked figure spread out on the bed, and knew that leaving him would be the hardest part. Even though the circumstances of their getting together had been led by her current situation, they had bonded together in a way she had not expected. To finally have found someone who "got her" and who was all that she had ever wanted...and to have to let all of that go. It was too cruel.

But she owed her life to Kathy, and would have never met Will in the first place if it wasn't for her sister. So she equalised and accepted what was about to happen. She would be strong, be brave, see this through to its end, no matter how bitter and hard that end would be.

Mel stubbed the cigarette out angrily on the balcony railing and crossed the room silently, the carpet warming her now-cold feet.

She opened the doors of the large built-in wardrobe, hoping to find a way to Narnia suddenly reveal itself, or a gateway to a different dimension at the very least. Sadly, it was just half-filled with her dresses and clothing. She selected an electric-blue mini skirt and check gingham blouse and placed them on the back of the chair, pausing to check the bags under her eyes in the dressing table mirror, before heading to the bathroom, and the comfortable sting of the power shower.

Will had woken when he heard the shower kick into life. He could hear Mel singing Amy Winehouse's *You know I'm no good* loudly in the shower and, on recalling the wild antics of the previous night, he was tempted to shout out "too bloody right" but he knew she probably wouldn't hear it.

He felt himself growing hard as he remembered how crazy she was last night, watching as she and Lucy dildo-ed each other, getting it on big time, as he and Guido double-teamed Jasmine, Dave having gone to bed, mumbling something about Jasmine giving him a 'sore arse' and being 'too old for all you beautiful young things.'

He knew that she was acting like that to squeeze every drop of fun into her last days of her life, or what she thought of as her last few days. He felt guilty almost immediately for not letting her in on his plan but he knew that she would have never gone along with it, there were way too many variables, and too much could go wrong. Mel would not risk her sister,s life on such a dangerous scheme, plus he had promised not to interfere with her plan.

All that said, he was not prepared to see her die, to let go of her so easily. Not now he had finally found someone who had bonded with him so quickly, who "got him" and was all that he ever had ever wanted. He would be strong and be brave, see this through to the bitter end, justifying breaking the promise he had made. He loved her too much to just stand by and watch her throw her life away.

He rose from the bed and headed towards the shower. Opening the cubicle door, he smiled at Mel, 'mind if I be no good with you?' and he stepped into her outstretched arms.

Kelly pulled up the driveway at the safe house in Swindon at six-thirty on Friday evening. She had dropped the twins off at Darren's at four and had swapped cars and outfits at the lock-up garage. She turned off Heart FM and stepped to the back of the car. The safe house was a semi-detached three story Edwardian in an affluent neighbourhood.

Her elderly neighbour waved and smiled as he clipped the privet hedge and she waved back. That was what she liked about this safe house. Everybody minded their own business and accepted her cover story that she worked for a merchant bank in New York so wasn't around much.

There was a gardener that came into do the garden once a week, a cleaner that came and cleaned once a week and Kelly turned up every now and again. This was one of three safe houses that she had. The others were in Manchester and Edinburgh, similar to this but this was her favourite and her South of England base. Barnaby owned them all but had chosen them with her assistance.

Most importantly, they all had large cellars that had been sound-proofed and extended out under the back gardens. Ideal for weapons concealment and testing.

She pulled her small luggage case from the small rear seat space. The case was empty except for her Kappa tracksuit and Reebok Classics, and the now dismantled Telinject Vario rifle, so she made a pretence of it being really, really heavy for her neighbours benefit.

She smoothed down her pinstripe business suit and extended the carrying handle, dragging the case theatrically up the drive as her high heels click-clicked on the tarmac.

Once inside, she disabled the alarms (including the special code for "Zone three", the cellar-door alarm system) checked the house, then returned to the case and picked it up easily and carried it along the hallway to the heavy wooden cellar door. She fished in her pocket for the large key. She had told the cleaner and the gardener that she had stored furniture down there and there was no need to enter. She also informed them that she had the only key and the cellar was on the alarm system. If either of them had felt nosey and forced the door, they would have been greeted by a whooping alarm and female voice informing them that the police had been called and this was an intruder alert.

In fact the alarm just tripped on Kelly and Barnaby's pagers to let them know that the house was compromised and it shut off automatically after two minutes. If the intruders hadn't shat themselves and legged it by then, opening the door at the bottom of cellar stairs without entering the correct code into the keypad on the entry panel would auto-initiate the phosphate and sulphur bombs in the cellar and wall linings, causing an instant inferno that would ignite the whole building. Very nasty, but very necessary.

Barnaby paid the cleaners and gardeners in all the safe houses well above the going rates, so had managed to avoid any awkward moments like this, so far anyway.

Kelly entered the cellar and opened the weapons locker that took up one wall of the small front cellar room, a box of about twenty feet long by ten feet high.

She pushed the heavy metal roller all the way back and surveyed the arsenal of death that decorated the walls.

What to use for a close-up job like this? How about my old Heckler and Koch USP copy? 9 mm, at close range, if I make up some Wildcat bullets and copper coat them, then they should pass straight through the skull and well out to sea, even with the silencer slowing things down, maybe...let's see if I can make this work.

Kelly lifted the dark metal semi-automatic pistol from the gun rack and headed towards the door leading to the firing range. She passed through and went straight to the CNC lathe and industrial drill that sat on one side of the room and fired them up. She had home made the pistol, which was based on the standard Heckler and Koch design but with her own "personal" modifications. Her home-made version was impossible to trace anyway, along with her "wildcat" bullets.

That was the one of the first things she learned from her dad,

'If you make the bullet yourself Kelly, and you make or modify the gun you fire it from yourself, who is going to know where it came from except you?'

She missed her dad so much, he always knew exactly what to do. And as she took measurements from the stripped-down gun, she heard his voice and got a memory of the smell of his coat again, causing her to stop for a moment and catch her breath. It was amazing how she could remember the smell of that coat, how her father would wrap her up inside it and carry her home when she would get too cold and sleepy.

It seemed like a whole lifetime ago to Kelly, so much had happened to her and changed her in the last ten years, so much pain and heartache, followed by the joy of the twins.

She wiped away a tear that had dropped from her face on to the matt-black metal of the pistol barrel and refocused her mind on the job in hand, pushing her emotions deep down inside, putting them into that dark corner of her psyche where she had learned to lock away all those childhood memories and feelings. She had noticed lately that these episodes of melancholy for her childhood were becoming more and more frequent.

Perhaps it's time for me to think about quitting this business, besides, I've got the girls future to think about now and they're getting more and more bloody inquisitive the older they get. Maybe one more year of cleaning and I'll call it day...yeah, find some nice bloke who'll be good to the girls and me, and settle into a nice comfy suburban existence.

As Kelly was working away in the cellar of the Swindon safe house, less than a hundred miles to the East of her, Will stood by the news kiosk at Paddington railway station.

Everything had gone as planned at the game that afternoon, he had already been to the bank to pay in his three-grand runners-up prize, and been to see Luke to thank him for setting up the meeting with Anton. He was confident that none of the SUBDL Officials had suspected anything as he was three sets to nil up on Anton when his game had deserted him anyway, and he lost the next five sets on the bounce. He didn't even have to try that hard to look exhausted and broken at the end of the game, the strain of the last fortnight's scheming, the fact that he always hated to lose a darts match, not to mention the heavy partying, were all starting to take their toll on Will both physically and mentally.

Even Soho Billy had given him a sympathetic pat on the back and refrained from his usual verbal sniping. He wouldn't miss the League and its pervading atmosphere of suppressed violence, always there and just bubbling below the surface. Neither would he miss the shitty venues and the constant reminders of his criminal past. But he was definitely going to miss the feeling of winning, some of the more colourful characters, the players, and being somewhat of a minor celebrity. Even if it was a celebrity status with a very limited audience and not something he could boast about to his mates down the pub.

He heard a 'Yo, man, you Will?' from behind him.

He spun around quickly.

Anton was right, despite the fact that Will had been nervously scanning the massive departure area at Paddington station, he had no idea where Derek had sprung from.

'Oh, hi, Derek right?'

Derek gave Will a smile that was full of gold teeth,

'Yes man, this is the book you order man.'

He handed Will a slightly distressed-looking paperback and quickly turned and walked away to mingle with the constantly moving river of commuters.

Will looked down at the paperback and smiled at Anton's little joke.

Derek had just handed him a tatty old copy of *The Great Escape* and a grimacing, defiant Steve McQueen stared out at him, trapped inside his barbed-wire prison of the front cover.

Once the train had pulled away from the platform he headed for the toilet with book and once inside, he checked through the book. The passports were inside an envelope that was taped to the back cover and when Will examined them they seemed like totally genuine UK passports, he couldn't tell the difference except that his name was now Andrew Robertson and his place of birth had changed from Chippenham to London. And he was eighteen months younger.

Mel was now Stephanie Evans, born in London and was just over a year younger.

Well, at least they didn't make her older, she's going to flippin' kill me! I'm not sure how she's going to take to being a 'Stephanie' either.

He pocketed the documents and headed back to his seat, thinking about the dangers the next forty-eight hours would bring for both of them.

Chapter Ten

Kelly kicked off her high heels and threw herself backwards onto the massive double bed. She had arrived at the holiday cottage at lunchtime on Saturday, after stopping off to pick up the keys from the letting agent in Seafordby. She had chosen the cottage from the brochure as it was at the quieter end of town and looked back across the bay towards the hotel from its elevated position. After walking through the holiday let to confirm all the access points and rear entrance to the property, she had gone to the large bay window at the front of the cottage and checked to see if "the impressive views of the bay and town of Seafordby" mentioned in the brochure, were as good as they claimed.

She could see the sales blurb hadn't been exaggerating for a change.

The Highcliff Hotel was clearly visible at the opposite end of the bay, its white walls glittering in the sunshine as the town spread out and down from it towards the bottom of the valley. The bay was almost a perfect "U" shape, with the two headlands mirroring each other, the sea sweeping between them to the crescent-moon shape of the sandy beach. The post equinox sunshine was beating down and the beach was busy with the weekend surfers, sand sailors, kite flyers and a smattering of families all enjoying the warmth of a sea that had been heated up by a long hot summer.

Barnaby was right, she thought to herself, *it is a lovely little place, the girls would love it down here. Bit worn and tacky in places but otherwise not half bad. Right then Kelly, that's enough of sea views, a visit to the hotel is next on the agenda!*

Four hours later on the other side of the bay, Mel stood on the balcony and looked across Seafordby to the holiday lets on the opposite headland and wondered how different this last fortnight might have been if she'd taken one of those cottages instead of staying at the hotel.

It would have been too quiet for me when I needed people to be around, plus I might not have met Will, although I was bound to find my way to the Blue Lagoon at some point.

Mel had become increasingly withdrawn over the last two days, despite Will's attempts to keep her entertained. It was as though she had fallen into a kind of trance, a quiet acceptance of the inevitable.

Will was worried by this change in her behaviour and had discussed the idea of letting her in on his plan with Dave, so worried was he by her depressed state.

Dave had advised him strongly that this would be a bad idea so he kept silent and continued to do his best to cheer Mel up, without much success.

Will stepped out onto the balcony and wrapped his arms around Mel, kissing the back of her neck gently as he did so.

'Hey, honey, let's just you and me go for a nice meal somewhere tonight yeah?'

Mel reached her hand back and softly stroked his cheek.

'Okay, Will, that sounds nice.'

Will hugged her closer.

'I want tonight to be special for you, Mel, we can do anything you want, anything at all.'

Mel turned to face him.

'I know, a quiet meal in a nice meal sounds perfect, then we'll see how I feel after that, it would be nice to go to Dave's for a bit as well to...you know, say goodbye...I suppose.'

Will leaned in closer and kissed her lips gently, amazed at how she always tasted of strawberries.

'Please don't think about goodbyes tonight, honey, we can just forget about tomorrow for one night and pretend the dawn won't arrive.'

Mel smiled and held Will closer,

'You can be quite poetic at times you know, when you put your mind to it. Yes...let's forget about tomorrow for one night, I'll just go and start getting ready.'

Will watched her retreat into the room and knew that above everything, he adored her completely and he was ready to give his life for her...or to take a life if it meant saving hers.

Mike polished the glass slowly, glancing at the small blonde in the business suit who sat among the other holidaymakers on the terrace sipping her orange juice with rapid, precise movements and returning the glass to the table with equal precision.

She looks a bit uptight, nice tits though, I might have to go and chat her up later if it quietens down a bit.

Kelly could see the barman checking her out in the corner of her eye.

If he doesn't stop staring at me I'm gonna go over and chin the fucker!

She stood up and casually moved to the far end of the sun terrace, adjusting her pink Gucci sunglasses and pretending to take in the views of Seafordby. She had already checked out the side of the hotel where the delivery area and staff entrance were on the left side of the building, and the cover was good there, not immediately visible from the main road either, gaining access through there would be easy enough. Turning slowly she studied the fourth floor, her gaze hidden behind the dark photo-chromic lenses, worked out which balcony was for room twenty-three from her mental map of the floor plan.

Hmm...that's about a seventy-foot drop through a toughened-glass roof, fuck me, I could hit the target with pillow and knock them over the railing and the fall would probably kill them.

That twat is staring at me again, time to move, Kelly...before you lose your temper with captain surf-tart, he is kinda cute though...still chin him for staring at me tits like that though.

Kelly moved back to the white plastic table, smiled at the two young children that were chasing each other in and out of the furniture, much to their parents' disapproval. She downed the remainder of her juice and walked towards Mike, holding the glass out to him as she approached him. She leaned in towards him as she passed and remarked quietly.

'You know, if you like my dress suit that much, I can get you a really good discount on one in your size, I'm sure they go all the way up to Orang-utan...ciao, baby!'

Mike's jaw dropped as Kelly placed the empty glass in his outstretched hand and sailed gracefully past him towards the lobby.

As she passed by the front desk she threw a quick glance at the corridor to the left of the desk which lead to the toilets and the entrance to the staff changing rooms, thought about going to pinch the chambermaid's uniform now, but reasoned somebody might report it missing before tomorrow night so she decided against it and carried on out of the hotel and into the warm October afternoon.

At eleven that night the Blue Lagoon was busy with weekend revellers

'So then my pretty, pretty...how's she bearing up?'

Dave patted the back of Will's hand and indicated to where Mel was sat, vacantly staring at the throng of bodies gyrating on the dance floor.

'Not good, mate, she's been really quiet, I just want this to be all over now. You need to run through the plan again?'

Will looked anxiously at Dave, who gave him a reassuring smile

'Stop worrying, sweetness! It's all in hand, you sneak me in the staff entrance while you two are in the bar and I go up to your room to wait for Mel to come up, simples!'

Will continued to frown.

'Yeah, simples. Provided she doesn't suss something's up

before then.'

'Look, honey, stop worrying and turn that frown upside down! Otherwise she will start to get suspicious.'

Dave pushed the two large tumblers of alcohol towards Will who managed to manufacture a grin.

'Yeah, right on the money as usual, Dave.'

'Uncle Dave knows best petal, now get over there and cheer up miserable Melanie!'

Will took the glasses and mouthed a thank you to Dave before heading towards where Mel was seated. The club was heaving with its normal Saturday night crowd and Will had already decided that keeping Mel away from the hotel for as long as possible was probably for the best tonight. He had a couple of the really good ecstasy pills left from their adventure earlier in the week, and they could take them to liven the night up a bit. Mel had cheered up a bit during the meal, helped along by cocktails and couple of bottles of red wine, but had almost burst into tears when she had seen Dave and seemed to fall back into her melancholic state.

She smiled sadly at Will as he sat down next to her.

'Here you go, honey, let's get this party started then!'

He palmed her the pill and held the drink out for her to take with her free hand.

Mel opened her palm to look at the pill, then swallowed it quickly, chasing it down with a large swig of her glass.

'Thanks, Will, just what the doctor ordered.'

Four hours later they sat huddled together on the beach, a large duvet that Will had taken from the linen room at the hotel wrapped around them both.

Mel leaned her head into Will's chest as she gazed out over the almost still water. There was almost no wind, but what breeze there was had a chill autumnal feel to it, and the only sound was the gentle whoosh of the waves as they caressed the sand of the beach.

'It's been a wonderful two weeks, Will, I couldn't have wished for a better holiday...or a better holiday companion than you.'

Will leaned his chin on the top of Mel's head.

'Shucks, honey, all part of the Highcliff Hotel's wonderful customer-service policy.'

Mel poked Will's stomach playfully.

'Why do you always have to be such as wise arse? You're spoiling my blissed-out nocturnal mood...dude.'

Will sniggered.

'See? ... Knew you'd pick up the local lingo eventually!'

'Yeah, I would've picked it up quicker if you lot didn't talk like you've got a mouthful of glue every time you speak, what's that accent all about?'

Mel looked mischievously at Will who feigned mock hurt.

'Huh! Just 'cause we bloody talk proper down yere!'

'What was that, something about tractors, I didn't quite catch it?'

It was Will's turn to poke Mel playfully in the ribs.

'That's enough of that city-girl! Behave or you won't get your Highcliff Hotel complementary sex on the beach.'

'Ooh! You rude bugger!'

The tickling fight started then, but it quickly developed into softer touches and whispers as they melted into each other's embrace.

Chapter Eleven

SUNDAY

Will toyed with his drink and looked at Mel as she tried to focus on the glass in front of her. They had been in the hotel bar drinking since lunchtime, pretty much from the time they had woken up. Will checked the digital clock on the wall as it clicked to eighteen-thirty and signalled at Mike to come over.

'I'm just popping to the loo, honey. Mike's coming over now'

Mel looked up at Will, her eyes red and puffy from crying.

She managed to squeak an 'okay' before lowering her head again and focused on just seeing one glass instead of two.

Will moved out of the bar and past the lobby where Ben looked up from his Star Trek Voyager annual and sneered at him.

'You still work here, baldy?'

'Go fuck yourself, you ginger freak'

Will didn't have time for this, he moved on down the corridor towards the toilets before Ben could respond. He swiped his electronic card in the lock and passed quickly through the changing room and along the back of the kitchen to the delivery entrance. He opened the door to be confronted by Dave wearing the most garish boating blazer that Will had ever seen.

'Fuck, Dave! You don't really get the phrase "low profile" do you?'

Dave feigned shock.

'I'll have you know this is the height of fashion in the Queens Road dahling! Besides, I made sure nobody saw me pull in here.'

'Good, here's the door pass and the mobile phone, I snuck up earlier and packed our bags, you remember where to plant the phone?'

Will was almost shaking with nervousness.

'Yes, yes...calm down, sweetheart, you'll have a heart attack. Don't worry, it will all be fine! Now here are my car keys, don't you dare damage my XJS, she's almost as precious to me as Guido, now run along back to Mel and I'll take care of the rest...and remember, keep calm and carry on.'

Dave gripped Will's shoulders with his two large hands and smiled at his friend.

Will looked at Dave and took a deep breath.

'Thanks, Dave, follow me, I'll show you where the laundry lift is.'

He led Dave to further along the wide corridor to the linen room and the large elevator where the hotels laundry was ferried to and from all floors.

He turned and gave Dave a hug before the large but colourfully dressed man stepped into the lift.

'Good luck, mate.'

Dave made a shooing motion with his hands and stepped into the lift, hitting the button for the fourth floor and folding his hands in front of him as he waited for the doors to close.

Will turned and headed back to the bar, the worried expression returning to his face.

Fernandez unlocked then opened the bottom-right drawer in his large desk, he removed the silver Glock and checked the magazine before replacing it in the grip and cocking the weapon.

How I loathe guns, so crude and instant, no style, no elegancia. However, Enrique, the cautious man is also the longest-lived.

He checked the document on the table in front of him and read it back to himself.

Repayment of one hundred and thirty thousand pounds to take place on Sunday the fourth of October, Highcliff Hotel, room twenty-three at seven-thirty pm, signed Will Cummings.

Fernandez picked up the document and walked to the filing cabinet. He opened it and went to 'C' in the alphabet before pulling out Will's file and replacing the document before pushing the drawer shut and locking the cabinet.

He scratched his head with the barrel of the gun before placing the heavy automatic into the pocket of his black jacket.

He hoped that Will would come up short on the money, he would enjoy going after Will's respectable parents to recoup the Organisation of Grey Fathers' losses.

A three for the price of one deal, a holy trinity of death, bueno!

Kelly parked the Audi three streets away from the hotel. She already checked out the route to the hotel the previous evening and had discovered that it took exactly seven minutes to walk at a brisk pace (and using a couple of access lanes that cut across the roads). She checked her watch.

'Seven minutes to walk, allow three for re-con and access to the staff area, five minutes find a uniform and get changed, then five to access the room, do the job and exit the building...that gives me five minutes to phone the girls and check that they're behaving themselves!'

Will leaned over to Mel and touched her lightly on the shoulder, he tried to keep his hand from trembling as she turned her tear-stained face towards him, her eyes wide, like a startled animal.

'Is it time?' she croaked hoarsely, her throat felt as dry as the Kalahari.

Will looked pained and pale.

'Yeah...seven-fifteen, hun, are you sure you don't want me to walk you to the room?'

'N...no, please...I'll just go, like we agreed, no fuss, just stay here.'

Mel touched Will's face gently and managed a smile, she rose and turned, walked unsteadily out of the bar towards the elevator.

It seemed as though she was sleepwalking or dreaming, and couldn't remember how she got there, but she was suddenly on the balcony of the room, looking out over Seafordby as the evening sky cast a deep blue glow over the bay.

She heard a noise from behind her and then a "click" as the lights in the room behind her were switched off. Mel braced herself for the impact, her hands reached forwards to grab the balcony rail as she prepared for the bullet, saying over and over in her mind, *please don't let it hurt! Please don't let it hurt!*

Then she felt a large hand clamp her across the mouth, a huge arm appeared from her left and clamped vice-like across her chest, pulling her backwards with such sudden force that she was too surprised to react.

She allowed herself to be dragged back across the room thinking all the while, *this isn't right...this wasn't how it was meant to happen!* She felt her legs turn to jelly and as though she was going to vomit, but then her fear began to change to confusion as she noticed a familiar smell of aftershave from her attacker, *where have I smelt that before?* She was hauled around the bed and into the large built-in wardrobe before being spun around to face a grinning Sinister Dave, his blue eyes twinkling in the dim half-light of the room.

Her eyes widened and she tried to cry out as Dave pushed her back amongst all her clothes and shoes, quickly pulling the wooden double doors closed behind him, barely squeezing his large frame into the space with Mel. He held his index finger up to his lips and whispered quietly,

'Sshhh, sweet-heart, watch and learn.'

Fernandez leant over and unzipped the small black bathroom bag on the passenger seat of the car, glancing up to keep one eye on the front entrance to the Highcliff as he did so, the bright spotlights positioned to illuminate the large Edwardian structure, as though it didn't already dominate its smaller residential neighbours enough. He took the thick cotton cloth out and placed it on his knee, before reaching into the bag again to remove the small bottle of chloroform. He doused the cloth thoroughly before placing both items quickly back into bag and zipping it up.

The priest looked up and saw a young blonde woman a few cars ahead of him check for traffic, re-adjust her shoulder bag before crossing the road, then head purposefully along the tarmac covered lane to one side of the hotel, and on down towards the hotel car park.

He checked his watch and still had a while. He could relax and compose himself until seven-twenty-five. He went over the plan again in his mind, if he was challenged when carrying an unconscious Will out of the building, he would simply say that Mr Cummings had suddenly felt unwell, and he was merely caring for one of his parishioners by ferrying him to the hospital. It had worked for him once before, there was no reason to think that it wouldn't work again.

Kelly searched through three lockers before she found a cleaner's house coat that fitted her well enough. She pulled it on over her black skirt and plain blue blouse and did up the buttons at the front. She had spent a couple of minutes in the car park, standing next to one of the half dozen cars in the car park and pretending to chat on her phone in case anyone emerged from the staff entrance. Kelly picked up her shoulder bag and headed along the corridor to the laundry room where she collected a linen cart and pushed it to the laundry elevator.

Once in the elevator, she opened her bag and took out the Heckler and Koch, quickly fixed the silencer to the pistol, then buried the bag in cart before covering the pistol with a towel so that it sat on top of the pile within easy reach.

As Kelly was slipping into the uniform, Fernandez crossed the road and headed into the hotel. He smiled and nodded at the ugly ginger desk clerk who had looked up from his comic book.

'One of your guests has requested some prayer and reflection on the Sabbath, my son, please do not trouble yourself, I have his room number it ees not necessary to escort me, he ees expecting me.'

Ben looked at the smiling priest.

'Oh right, okay, go ahead, Father, no worries.'

'Thank you, my friend, have a good evening.'

He watched as the priest walked to the elevator and summoned the lift, he shuddered before going back to his comic, priests always gave him the creeps, *all that kiddy-fiddling business, weirdo's!*

Fernandez hummed lightly as he travelled upwards and exiting the lift on the fourth floor he checked his gold Rolex, *seven-twenty-six, time is up, Mister Cummings!*

He headed along the corridor, counting the room numbers off before arriving at number twenty-three. As he knocked on the door it swung ajar slightly so he pushed against it to open it wider,

'Hello? Will, my friend?'

The room was dark so he felt for the light switch before entering through the door, he sensed that something felt wrong about this so he reached inside his coat pocket to grip his Glock firmly, ready to draw it out. The fingers of his left hand found the light switch and he flicked it on.

In the wardrobe, Mel and Dave gave a sharp intake of breath simultaneously as the light streamed through the latticed wooden slats of the door.

Fernandez entered the room cautiously and closed the door behind him.

'Will, my friend, stop playing games with me and show yourself!'

He scanned the room and headed towards the wardrobe.

As she saw the shadowy outline move towards the wardrobe door Mel tensed and felt like screaming, she couldn't understand any of this, *who was this guy and why was he asking for Will? And what the fuck was Dave doing here?*

As Fernandez reached for the door handle of the wardrobe a loud familiar Nokia ringtone broke the silence and Fernandez stopped and froze. He turned and walked around the bed towards the balcony where the ringing seemed to be coming from.

His immediate thought was *bomb?* And he could almost feel the adrenalin levels pumping through him jump through the roof.

Surely this Cummings was too small fry to be involved with explosives and bombs, unless Winters had lied? No...Winters was too frightened of being discovered, he could not risk such a thing, this was a stupid game that Cummings was playing with him to avoid payment!

He stepped out on the balcony and saw the phone buzzing and ringing in the pot plant he reached down and picked up the phone.

He clicked the green button and put the phone to his ear.

'Hello?'

'Hello, Father, I'm down here...'

Fernandez moved towards the balcony rail and looked down to the floodlight terrace below.

Will was stood at one end of the terrace and waving up at the priest.

'I do not appreciate your stupid game, Will, I would, however, appreciate eet if you would come up here and give me my money young man!'

Fernandez had recovered his composure now and didn't hold back on the bile in his tone.

'Oh, you'll get it, Father'

Will looked at his watch and paused as it clicked over to seven-thirty.

'Right about now I shouldn't....'

Kelly pulled the cart to a halt outside room twenty-three and checked her watch,

'Seven-twenty-nine, time for work,' she murmured quietly.

She could hear a man's voice from inside the room and reached under the towel for the pistol. She clicked the safety off and checked along the corridor in both directions before pulling the gun out and swiping the electronic door pass at the same time.

As the door clicked open she pushed it wide quickly and stepped into the room in one smooth movement.

Fernandez spun around as he heard the door open, the phone still up against his ear and was baffled by the sight of the small blonde girl he had seen earlier, now dressed as a cleaner, levelling the silenced pistol up and pointing it straight at him.

Oh goody! A priest, fuckin' pervs! Isn't suicide a sin though? Oh well, takes all sorts I spose, thought Kelly as she pulled the trigger and watched as the priest's head flew back and he disappeared over the balcony, knocked backwards by the force of the bullet.

She waited a second or two for the loud bang which echoed through the open window as Fernandez's body hit the safety glass of the terrace roof, then she turned, pulled the door closed behind her and replaced the gun back under the towels before trundling the laundry cart quickly back towards the lift.

Will didn't have time to finish his sentence before he saw Fernandez turn, then he heard a pop, and watched as Fernandez toppled backwards over the balcony rail and hit the glass roof headfirst, before sliding off forwards to land on the concrete terrace. He walked over to the priest's body. He was almost unrecognisable as the impact had caved in the top part of his head and bits of brain and skull were splattered on the terrace.

Will threw up a bit of sick and then opened Fernandez's hand, removed the mobile phone that the dead man was still gripping tightly and slipped it into his pocket. He reached into the priest's pocket and found the heavy Glock. He transferred it to his own pocket and then found the small black case in the other pocket.

He knew that he didn't have much time before people came running so quickly pocketed the case and searched for any other incriminating evidence. He was hoping to find the copy of their agreement, he found Fernandez's car keys and wallet, replaced them quickly but there was no sign of the document.

It must still be in his office at the church...

He heard a gasp from above and looked up to see Dave and Mel standing together on the balcony, a look of horror and anger on Mel's face. He gave them a quick wave and a thumbs-up signal before he ran to the side of the terrace and hopped over the metal railing to head around the outside of the hotel towards the car park. As he reached the corner of the building he looked back to see Ben and Mike standing over the broken body of Fernandez. He turned away from the scene and rounded the corner of the Hotel before crossing the car park quickly and unlocking the XJS.

The next two minutes seemed to take forever before Mel and Dave emerged from the staff entrance and Will quickly moved towards Mel.

She broke away from Dave's grip and rushed towards him landing a punch on the jaw and then launching wildly at him with punches and kicks as Will tried to get hold of her.

Then he managed to wrap his arms around her to stem the flurry of blows.

'Bastard! Fucking bastard fucker! Bastard! You promised! ... You promised me...bastard!'

Her curses which had started as shouts, diminished to breathless croaks interspersed with sobs, as her attack ran out of steam and

the tears began to flow.

Will waited for her to calm down before he said.

'I'm sorry, honey, it was the only way I could get the money for your sister and keep you alive.'

Mel froze and searched Will's face, she was confused, shocked and trembling, the execution of Fernandez playing over and over in her mind like a stuck record.

'What? But h...how?'

Will smiled and kissed her forehead

'I'll explain it all when we get to Dave's but we have to leave, and leave now, before the old bill arrive.'

Will nodded at a pale and grim-faced Dave.

'Let's get outta here, mate.'

Chapter Twelve

Rob Winters was still tailing the fat man in the Mercedes when the call came in over the police radio.

A sudden death at the Highcliff Hotel of an unidentified male. Rob's mind began racing immediately...*I bet that stupid fucker Fernandez went too far this time and offed Cummings...and I expect he'll want me to cover up his bastard mess!*

When he saw the body of Fernandez he got on to the office straight away.

'Hi Tom, it's Rob Winters here, I need S.O.C.O. and you to get here double quick, I've got to follow up a lead from one of the witnesses before the trial goes cold. I've called the Doc and secured the crime scene, there's a uniform unit here but I need you up here to question the rest of the witnesses.'

'Are we looking at foul-play boss?'

The Detective Sergeant could barely contain the excitement in his voice, hopefully a juicy murder that would put this little shithole on the map!

'Not sure, Tom, it's probably a suicide but I need to check this lead out first, just get here quick.'

As soon as he got off the phone, Rob switched on the siren and drove to St. Francis at breakneck speed.

He pulled into the car park and turned off the engine, that was when he noticed his hands were shaking. He felt the familiar tightness in his chest and quickly stepped out of the car and went to the trunk of the car. He knew what had to do to save his career, marriage, everything.

He lifted the green metal petrol can from the trunk and closed it before striding across to the church. The whole building was in darkness and Winters knew that the housekeeper would have left at seven thirty and locked up after the last Sunday service at six pm.

He had to break in at the side entrance to the presbytery behind the church and quickly headed for Fernandez's office.

He searched the office frantically for the cellar keys but gave up quickly when they didn't materialise. A quick search of the kitchen revealed a hammer and cold chisel from a tool box at the back of a small larder.

After breaking the cellar door he made his way to Fernandez's torture room, doused the room with half the petrol can before igniting a piece of cloth and heading back up to the office.

After breaking open the filing cabinets and desk drawers and throwing the contents around the room he searched for a safe or security box but could find no evidence of one. He found a couple of blank computer discs in one of the desk drawers and pocketed them, hoping that they were what he was looking for. He didn't have time to check them now, he had to act fast.

He doused the study with the rest of the petrol, stepped back to the doorway before lighting a piece of paper and throwing it into the room, making sure the fire caught hold before he turned and ran back down the hallway.

As he ran and rounded the corner by the presbytery entrance he collided and bounced off Will Cummings running in opposite direction, the impact knocking both of them off their feet and onto the stone tiles of the corridor.

Rob got to his feet first and offered his hand to a shocked and winded Will.

'It's okay, Mr Cummings, we better get out of here, fast.'

Will recovered himself slightly.

'Who the hell are you?'

'Detective Inspector Winters, pleased to meet you, I'll explain later, come on, son, up you get, time to move.'

Will took the outstretched hand and allowed Winters to haul him up. He was just about to ask Winters what the hell was going on when there was a loud crash followed by a noise that sounded like "WHOOPMFF".

'Come on, kid, move your arse, this whole place is going up.'

Will allowed the policeman to push him and they both ran through the side door.

Once they got outside to the pathway leading to the car park Will looked backed and could see the flames and thick black smoke escaping from one side of the building.

'Fuck me! Did you just do that? I...I don't get this!'

Winters was bent double and breathing hard.

'It's okay, kid, I know you owed Fernandez and believe me, he would have killed you if you hadn't paid up.'

The policeman straightened up and coughed.

'You best make yourself scarce, son, I take it you'll be leaving Seafordby for...somewhere safer?'

Will nodded, confused and shocked by the events of the last few minutes.

'Yeah...but, I mean...why? What's your connection with Fernandez?'

'Long story, kid, but let,s just say I won't be mourning the fucker's passing. And don't worry about this, I'll come up with something.'

Winter's turned to see how quickly the fire was taking hold and then turned back to Will.

'You best get going now, son, I'm about to call this in...oh, and by the way, we never met and this conversation never happened, clear?'

Will looked at the rapidly spreading fire then back to sombre and serious looking policeman. He said one word before turning and breaking into a sprint for the car park,

'Crystal.'

He started the XJS and drove as fast as he could to The Blue Lagoon.

By the time he got there, Dave had explained to Mel how the money from Fernandez was in his account just waiting to be transferred to Mel's sister's account and as it was a charitable donation no one would even raise an eyebrow.

Mel was still mad with Will, and Dave, but had calmed down slightly after a couple of large glasses of Chivas Regal.

She looked up angrily at Will as he walked through the door into the club.

'So what's next then, genius? We all go to prison for a few years for murdering a priest?'

Will smiled and held up his hands in surrender.

'Whoa there, tiger! We're going to have to take a little trip yes, but prison? No way, honey, I've been there and done that and I've got no intention of going back there. But you better finish that drink up cause we're leaving...now'

Kelly sipped at a can of lager as she watched the flashing blue lights reflecting off the white façade of the hotel on the other side of the bay. As she pulled the towelling dressing gown closer around her chest and leaned against the frame of the bay window, she noticed that there were more blue lights heading towards the top of the town where there seemed to be a large fire burning out of control.

'Hmm, wonder what that's all about?'

She reached into the pocket of her dressing gown, fished out her mobile phone and punched the speed dial for Barnaby. She waited for a couple of rings before he answered.

'Hello, Kelly, my dearest, how are you?'

'Fine thanks Mr B, job done, you were right about this being a nice place as well. I think I might even bring the twins down here next summer.'

'Ah yes, the pleasures of the English seaside town, delightful! I trust there were no complications with the job?'

Barnaby eased further down on the black leather sofa and gazed into the mock electric fire that was throwing glimmering patterns around his dimly lit lounge.

'Nope, bit surprised it was a priest though, first time I've ever popped a clergyman.'

Barnaby's hand shook and a large splash of Burgundy escaped the wine glass he was holding and fell onto his ludicrously expensive Persian rug.

He sat bolt upright in his seat. A bead of sweat formed on his upper lip and his heart rate jumped up to double its normal rate.

'Did you just say "priest"?'

'Yeah, Spanish-looking, late thirties or early forties, why?'

Barnaby thought for a moment, *what was a priest doing connected with Ray in Ibetha? A priest committing suicide? Something is not right here. But she said he looked Spanish? Maybe it's kosher, I'll make a phone call tomorrow just in case.*

'Oh, nothing, my dear, I'm afraid I just spilt a rather good drop of Burgundy on my Persian rug, I'd better go see to it. I'll call you tomorrow morning, my dear. Sleep well.'

'Riiight...whatever Barnaby, speak to you tomorrow.'

Kelly disconnected the call and tapped her chin with the mobile phone.

'Hmmm, well that was a bit weird...never mind, Kelly. Bedtime girl! Long drive back tomorrow.'

Rob Winters watched as the fire brigade tried its best to bring the fire under control. They were fighting a losing battle as the whole building was now ablaze. A medium-sized crowd had gathered to watch the excitement and he watched as the detective sergeant pushed his way through a group of gawking teens, stepped under the police tape that the uniformed unit had rapidly thrown across the entrance to the car park.

He nodded to approaching detective.

'Tom, anything new on our hotel body?'

'Not much, boss, the forensics guys think it's probably suicide but it's too early to tell yet. This is a bit of a blaze innit? You knew it was Father Fernandez from the I.D. In the wallet yeah?'

Winters shrugged.

'How many priests are there in Seafordby? I just put two and two together. This place was on fire when I got here, I'm guessing our victim started it. I managed to get inside and tried to check if anyone was in there but the fire had taken hold too quickly so I had to make a rapid exit. Any idea what he was doing at the hotel?'

The detective sergeant shook his head.

'The receptionist said that Fernandez told him he was visiting a parishioner who was staying at that the hotel but he didn't give a name of who he was visiting. Nothing to go on from the body, he still had his wallet and car keys so robbery is out. Uniform are still taking statements but I've said we'll interview the all of the staff tomorrow.'

'Any staff or guests missing?'

Tom consulted his notebook.

'No guests, but one member of staff who was drinking in the bar just before it happened. A Will Cummings. Apparently he's on annual leave at the moment but sometimes drinks in the bar. The barman said he left the hotel five minutes before Fernandez arrived and the receptionist backed that up. I've got an address for him, want me to check him out?'

Winters shook his head.

'Naw, leave that one to me, I'll go round there later tonight and get a statement.'

Tom shrugged.

'Okay, I'll get off then. Goodnight boss.'

Winters nodded and kicked idly at the gravel and then looked up to watch his handiwork with inner satisfaction.

'Goodnight, Tom.'

Yeah, goodnight, not a bad night at all.

I suddenly feel warm all over...

Two days later, Mel and Will stood at the rear of the ferry and watched as the white Dover shoreline faded into the distance.

Mel turned to Will and nudged his elbow.

'So then, Andrew Robertson, run it by me again, how much money have we got and why are we going to Estonia?'

Will smiled and looked down at the churning white wake being thrown out by the powerful propellers of the ferry.

'Well, Stephanie Evans, as I've already explained, we have about sixty grand in the bank under my new name and Estonia is one of the only countries in Europe that does not have a Catholic diocese within its borders. In fact the last time I checked less than one percent of the population is Catholic and it's ranked as the second-least religious country in the world, only beaten by China, it's also quite a funky little country. If a little cold in the winter. They score pretty highly on the happiness scale, probably because they don't have all those paranoia's and hang-ups caused by religion. So my studies in European History came in handy after all.'

'I thought that Tallinn was full of boozy Brits on stag and hen dos?'

Will nodded.

'True enough, that's why we're not going to Tallinn, were going to the university city of Tartu in the south of the country.'

'Okay, but what about the police, wont they investigate why the priest was in my room and why we have both disappeared?'

Will shook his head and smiled at Mel.

'Nope, according to the computer records of the hotel you checked out of that room on Sunday morning and I handed my notice in on Friday, told the boss I had an offer of a bar job in Spain. Besides, I think the friendly policeman I told you about is not going to be digging too deep into the case. The main thing is we're together, your sister can get her treatment and we're about to embark on an adventure in a new country.'

Mel pulled Will close to him and gave him a hug.

'Yeah, alright, Mr Robertson, smarty-pants. It looks like you covered all the angles... I've not forgiven you yet, though. You're got a lot of making up to do, "Andrew". I'm not sure if I'm totally happy about being a "Stephanie" yet, I always fancied myself as a "Sophia", much more exotic!'

Mel watched as the coastline dissolved into a hazy blur and thought that summed up her thoughts about the last three days. It had all been a hazy blur, but she was alive, and with her lover.

And that had to be a good thing.

She looked up at Will.

'Fancy a game of darts? I noticed a dartboard in the bar.'

Will laughed and leaned in to kiss Mel.

'Why not, Miss Evans. Let's play darts!'

Preview of "Kelly's Eye"

The action-packed sequel to "Underclass" – Available in 2013

Kelly's phone rang just as she was leaving the shed in the garden of the safe house in Manchester. The late April sunshine was beating down and it made a nice change from the usual Manchester rain. She was still going over the events of the previous night before phoning Barnaby. It had been a bit of a mess really but Kelly knew she had been sloppy. She had been in the empty office block four times before the hit and not run into anyone.

Kelly had completed the straightforward hit on the businessman who, until an hour ago, was sitting quietly at his desk half a mile away from the empty office block that Kelly had set up in when the high velocity bullet punched through the glass.

The bullet then travelled through his head and buried itself at the base of the wall behind him and Kelly packed her rifle into the holdall and headed for the staircase.

She had stopped in her tracks halfway down the stairwell between the sixth and fifth floors when the security guard had stepped onto the stairwell from the fifth floor and then froze as he looked up at her.

He had got as far as 'What the fu...' before she had drawn the pistol and fired, hitting him square between the eyes.

She felt terrible immediately.

'He wasn't supposed to be there!'

She kept repeating this between sobs as she drove back to the safe house. He was on duty half an hour early and the security sweep of the empty office block wasn't due for another hour.

'What the fuck was he doing there?' she sobbed as she turned into the street where the safe house was located. Kelly had never killed a bystander before. Barnaby had warned her that one day she might have to kill a witness, but had always planned so carefully to avoid any innocent party that she could hardly believe what had happened.

After a sleepless night it was a very weary Kelly that pulled the mobile from the pocket of her jeans. After wiping a tear from her eye she tried to compose herself when she looked down and saw that it was Darren, her ex on the phone.

'Hi Darren, how are the girls?'

'What the fuck have you been up to!!! You fucking bitch!!'

Darren was screaming down the phone at her.

'You what? Darren! For fuck's sake! Calm down and tell me what's happened.'

'You tell me you fucking bitch! The school just phoned and said a policeman and a nun...a fucking nun! They just picked the girls up from the school, said they had a court order and were taking them into care, and...get this right, they want to talk to you! Mind tellin' me what's going on? Eh? Cause I phoned the fucking Willow Trees and they said you were on leave for the weekend! What the fuck is going on Kelly? ... Kelly? Answer me!

Kelly dropped the phone and sank onto the grass as the shock hit her.

They've found out...they've found out about Fernandez...

Roundfire Books put simply, publish great stories. Whether it's literary or popular, a gentle tale or a pulsating thriller, the connecting theme in all Roundfire fiction titles is that once you pick them up you won't want to put them down.